Written by...

Carmen L. F. Wong

For book orders, email orders@traffordpublishing.com.sg

Most Trafford Singapore titles are also available at major online book retailers.

Printed in Singapore.

ISBN: 978-1-4669-3178-7 (sc)
ISBN: 978-1-4669-3179-4 (hc)
ISBN: 978-1-4669-3180-0 (e)

Trafford rev. 04/12/2013

T**ff**ord www.traffordpublishing.com.sg

Singapore
toll-free: 800 101 2656 (Singapore)
Fax: 800 101 2656 (Singapore)

To Joshua & Jacob

Acknowledgement

Thanks to Professor Kit Kelen. Without you, the story might never be developed into words on pages. Thanks for your patience and encouragement to urge me on and guide me through those moments of doubts and difficulties.

Thanks to MAC and all my students. You are my source of inspiration and motivation. You enlightened me with creativity, imagination, courage and passion. I hope we can all keep that light on, to inspire and be inspired, to motivate and be motivated.

Thanks to Joshua, my first reader. Your passion to read encourages me to write. Having my book on your shelf has always been an essential driving force. Thanks to Jacob, a great fan to my spontaneous stories. Your enjoyment of the stories empowers me to create.

Thanks to my parents. 感謝爸爸媽媽。沒有用上您們能明白的文字寫一本書， 也甚少把感謝的說話宣之於口， 但由衷的為您們對我所負出的一切無言感激。

Contents

1

Are you ready for our new story?

'Are you ready for our new story tonight?' Gavin was just laying Zoe down on the bed. This was after the piggy back ride that she'd won by brushing her teeth nicely.

'It's a long one this time so . . .'

'O! I like a long story,' the high spirited Zoe interrupted, 'I am sure I can stay awake as long as I need to.'

'No, the reason I'm saying it is because we'll only read the first chapter tonight.'

'Oh! . . . Daddy, what about two chapters? Please.' Zoe pleaded. She would never give up without trying though she didn't expect her dad would say yes this time.

'No,' Gavin was firm. He knew how five minutes became ten minutes with Zoe and then ten minutes became fifteen minutes. He wished he was as determined as his daughter.

Gavin got his laptop and began the story. 'The story was called "Long and the Magic Feather"'.

Once upon a time in the early Ming Dynasty of China, there lived a talented young artist called Long. He'd showed his talent in drawing since he was only three. Long's father would have wished to see the boy grow into a great artist one day but the old man died when Long was only eight. After that, his mother had to work hard to raise him. They were so poor that they could not even afford a proper paintbrush. While others drew with paintbrushes of wolf fur or rabbit fur, Long's mother made him a paintbrush with her own hair. They couldn't afford to buy ink or paper either so Long practised drawing with water on the only wooden table at home. So images of hills and streams, flowers and trees, fish and birds, and even people at a glance, had to be first captured into his mind. From Long's memory, people and nature came to life again on that old broken table, even if it was for just an instant. It wasn't just that he never missed the details or the spirit, Long was also quick to make sure he had the whole picture before the wet image faded.

Long's mother was the only person who showed appreciation and admiration for his drawings. But not long after he turned fifteen, his mum got very sick. A few months later the creditors came to take away their house, including of course the only wooden table. Two days later, his mum died and he felt sorry that she couldn't even take her last breath under her own roof. A proper burial would be the last and only thing he could offer her.

For three days and nights, on the main street of Nanjing[1], the capital city, Long wore a sign begging every person passing by to hire him to drawing portraits for them. It was cold so there were not many people on the street. Wealthy people were riding in sedan chairs with drawn

---

[1]   Nanjing was still the capital of the Ming Dynasty during the early years of Emperor Yongle. It was in 1403 that Yongle demoted Nanjing as a secondary capital and announced Beijing as the new capital.

curtains. Occasionally, some did throw him a coin just as they did for other beggars, but no one stopped for a portrait. Most people walking by were working or in a hurry to get somewhere. Some threw a contemptuous or indifferent glance at Long in his shabby clothes and then they went on their way. Some did show pity but who among these people having to work outdoors on such cold days had an extra coin to give. They could only give him advice, 'Go home, young man. Just dig a hole for your dead mum. She won't feel the cold anyway.'

It was the third day and it began to snow. Long had just a few coins. People's indifference chilled him more than the icy wind. But it was in that loneliest and coldest winter he had ever experienced, Long did meet two nice people who warmed his heart again. Long was standing with his sign outside a big mansion. A sedan chair stopped in front of it and out stepped a noble lady and her daughter who was almost of Long's age. Before they reached the house, they spotted the indigent youth shivering in the cold wind.

'Young man, it's so cold and it's getting dark. What are you standing here for?' The lady spoke to him gently.

'My dear lady, my mum died three days ago and I've tried to earn some money to get her buried properly. Getting her a simple, crude coffin and a plot dug deep enough to keep her from the wild animals. That was my only wish. For as much as you are ready to pay, I could draw . . . . ,'

"She put the money in Long's freezing hands."

Before he finished, the lady had already indicated for her attendants to fetch her a string of coins. She put the money in Long's freezing hands. 'Don't worry, young man, . . .' she began coughing after saying just a few words. She knew she wouldn't have the strength to finish her comforting line so she just ended it with a smile.

After all his trouble, it was beyond Long's dreams to get that amount and with the money in his hands he burst into tears. 'Th-th-thank you ve-ve-ry much,' stuttered the sobbing Long.

Long tried to look away in embarrassment but felt even worse when he caught sight of the young girl who was standing by the lady's side. He could see that her big sparkling eyes were fixed on his mortified look. A smile flickered across her rosy, dimpled cheeks as she tried to hold back her laughter. She was holding out her handkerchief to Long, and encouraging him to make use of it. Long took the handkerchief and the girl blushed as her eyes met his.

In the meantime, the attendants were hurrying the lady to go back to the house and get out of the cold. The young girl offered her arm as a support and the two of them now wobbled towards the door.

Long wiped away his tears and remembering something, he rushed to catch up with them. 'There's little that I could do, my dear lady, but if you could spare some of your precious time, I would like to make a portrait of you in return as my gratitude for your kindness.' Long's eyes were full of sincerity.

The lady waved her hand gently to decline the offer with a forced smile and a feeble shake of her head. Long lowered his head in embarrassment as he felt one more blow of rejection.

The lady tapped Long gently on his shoulder. After a fit of coughing, she re-assured him, 'I believe you are a good artist. You mother must be very proud of you . . . but it's late now. You will have a chance when I get stronger after this cold winter is over.'

Long looked at her face which was as pale but as gentle as the moonlight reflected in the snow. Her face reminded him of his dead mother's. He wouldn't forget it. He promised to himself that one day he would draw a portrait for her and for his mother that would revive their beauty from the tortures of sickness. Long nodded hard to show his determination.

'Now go home and have a good rest. You still have a long road in front of you. Your mother could rest in peace only if she could see her child living on bravely and in good health.' As she struggled to speak to Long between the coughs, the lady also took a glance at the little girl who was by her side, gently patting her back. Long followed her glance and saw tears welling up in the girl's eyes.

A minute ago she'd been smiling, now her rosy cheeks were pale as the lady's and her two big eyes rolling around as she tried to stop her tears. Long moved a step toward her, wishing that he could comfort her but what was he going to say? He hesitated and stopped there, 'thank you very much, good bye.' Then he turned and left, his heart warmed in the cold wind as he walked on with the coins in his pocket, the girl's handkerchief in his hand and the mother and daughter in his mind.

Zoe had been listening attentively as if she was just around the corner of that main street to peep and eavesdrop on the whole scene. She felt angry as the people walked away from Long with indifference, sad as Long shivered helplessly in the cold, touched when the lady put money in Long's hands. And now she was of course expecting a romance as Long walked away with the girl in his mind. It was when Gavin stopped the story that Zoe found herself back in her bed.

'That's it?' Zoe asked, disappointed.

'Yes, enough for tonight.'

'What will happen next? . . . Will Long meet the girl again? . . . . Will they fall in love and live happily forever and ever? . . . Will the lady die? . . .' Zoe was curious and persistent.

Gavin knew that he couldn't give an answer to any question then or it would invite more. Now the only thing he could do was to give a command, 'Close your eyes and sleep now!'

'Errrrrrrrr . . . .'

'We will continue tomorrow if you sleep now, learn well in school and eat a good dinner tomorrow.' Gavin tucked Zoe in bed and kissed her gently on her forehead. 'Sleep tight, sweetie. You may dream about it.'

'Good-night daddy! Don't stay up too late.'

This was the most comforting moment of the day when Gavin watched his beloved daughter falling into sleep so peacefully and securely. How could he have missed it during her first three years?

But he knew why it had been that way. Accidents happen 24 hours a day and the patients needed him. That was Gavin's reason during those times when he was a hardworking emergency room surgeon. Even when he was on a day shift, he would be busy reading medical journals in his study after dinner. Of course it was only possible for Gavin to maintain such a total commitment to his profession because he had a capable and understanding wife. Sofia managed the family and the young daughter well. Gavin thought he would have the time to make up when he had his own practice. Then one day she was diagnosed with cancer of the pancreas and a few months after the diagnosis and the torturing chemo treatment, the cancer cells had spread to the liver. Things went rapidly downhill after that.

Gavin quit the job that made him regret the loss of time. He'd started making up fairy tales at Sofia's bedside in the hospital as a way to cheer her up. The stories energized her to visualize herself as a brave princess fighting against the cancer monster. Gavin was a surgeon but surgery would be of no use and neither were the medicine or chemotherapy that he and

Sofia chose to try. It was Gavin's stories or maybe his total devotion of time that relieved her from the nauseating side effects. This gave her the courage to fight back for a few more months in the face of death and pain. Sofia died when Zoe was only four.

Even after the funeral, Gavin did not return to medicine. He was afraid to miss moments he could share with his daughter just as he had missed so much with his wife. Some saw his ditching his career as atonement. Others viewed it as a sacrifice. Gavin didn't feel he was doing either of those things.

Gavin enjoyed every moment spent for and with Zoe, writing for her, cooking for her, ironing her clothes, playing with her and teaching her, answering her thousands of questions, reading to her and listening to the stories she made up. He loved her above everything and was grateful to have this angel in his life.

Gavin enjoyed his work now as a freelance fairy tale writer. He used to love fairy tales when he was young and was grateful that some of his childhood fairy friends must have stayed on in his brain to keep his stream of imagination flowing. And that he was making a living from this work, he felt satisfied to bring dreams to the children. By recalling his own childhood and looking at Zoe's expression when she read or listened to his stories, Gavin could feel how some, if not most, children would be caught in the fascination. He believed that one day, this experience of fantasy might help them to create their world or at least face reality from another perspective.

From time to time, Gavin still missed his wife but he was grateful to have started a new chapter in life.

2

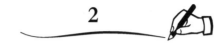

We will have the time

Gavin had been busy the whole morning with the house chores, which he enjoyed because, like everything he did, he was doing it for Zoe. In the afternoon, he returned to his computer and had just finished the second chapter. He read it through again.

After his mother's burial, Long soon found a job as a house servant for a rich merchant, Li. He received no payment but just three meals and a place to stay. Like all the junior servants, he had to wake up earlier than anyone else and start getting the fire in the kitchen ready before sunrise. At night time, he would be one amongst the last to check everything before he could go to bed. Work was tough but he liked the place since there were beautiful paintings hanging all around. It was a rich collection of paintings from various artists through which his master could show off his admiration of the arts. Long was much inspired in the environment but as a servant, he never made any comments on the paintings. He just dreamt that one day he could have his own paintings hanging in his admirers' houses.

Written by...

Long always kept his mother's paintbrush and the girl's handkerchief in his pocket. They became his source of inspiration. Every time he touched the two treasures in his pocket, he would whisper in his heart. *I promise I will become a great artist one day.*

Long couldn't leave the house as he wished but when he was asked to fetch something on the main street, he would deliberately take the long route to walk past that big mansion. One time, Long did see the girl again on the street but he felt too inferior to approach her or talk to her. Still, from her smiling face, he knew that her sick mother was fine, at least for that day. At that moment, Long just wished that he could have the chance to see the girl and her smile from time to time, even if it was from a distance.

Then one day, Master Li ordered, 'Get prepared for a big feast tonight! We will watch the moon and the chrysanthemums in the garden. Master Sun may come as well.'

Long knew it would be a busy day again but he was used to this since his master enjoyed inviting his artist and poet friends to his garden to celebrate the blooming of different kinds of flowers at different seasons. This time Li was particularly excited because Master Sun, the famous traveling artist was in the city and it would be such an honour to have him accepting the invitation.

That night while the host and guests were appreciating the beauty of the chrysanthemums under the autumn moon, Long suddenly felt the desire to draw. While the guests were drawing with ink on paper, Long drew with water on the granite floor next to the well where he was supposed to be washing the dishes.

Master Sun was finding his way back to the main garden after taking a wrong turn, when he happened to walk by the washing area. He saw Long moving swiftly around the well, bending down here and there with something that looked like a paintbrush in his hand. Sun was curious about what Long was doing. He got closer and caught sight of the moon's reflection on the granite floor. Then he saw pictures of blooming chrysanthemums drawn reflected in the wet surface. He was amazed by the subtlety and liveliness of the picture he saw, particularly when he considered that it was drawn with no ink, but just water.

'Excellent!' exclaimed Sun, 'It seems you have planted the most charming chrysanthemums in the stone. With these blossoms posing gorgeously over the reflection of the moon, I'm sure those in the garden would rather wish the moon was hidden behind the clouds.'

Long was so immersed in his drawing that he hadn't realized the famous artist Sun was standing behind him until he heard the exclamation. Courteously, he turned and bowed to greet him, 'Good Evening, Master Sun. Is there anything that I could do to help you?'

'Yes, just continue with your drawing,'

'But it's done.' Long replied timidly.

'I mean on a piece of paper.' Sun was assuming what he saw on the ground was a draft ready to be transferred.

'I haven't been able to afford any paper or ink so I've got used to drawing on the ground or the table with water.' Long explained.

'It's such a pity!' Sun gave a slight sigh as he watched the picture fading away.

'Just some scribbles.' Long was trying to be humble. But actually his heart was overjoyed by the compliment, especially since it was from a great artist. His heart was now burning with the passion to create and draw again.

Sun's heart was also burning but, with the fire of jealousy. Still he was able to hide his emotion under his laughter. 'Scribbles! . . . Ha! Ha! . . . Interesting! I really envy your talent, young man. Your scribbles can sell for a high price. Ha! Ha! But of course that would be when you become well known.' Sun knew in his heart that this young boy's talent and skill would outstrip his.

After his comments, Sun turned and was ready to go. Long should just say goodnight to end the conversation but he couldn't hold his tongue. Long would like to be a great artist like Master Sun. He took a deep breath and holding the paintbrush and handkerchief in his pocket for support, Long knelt before Sun. He bowed and begged Sun to take him as an apprentice.

'Master Sun, I like your pictures very much. Would you please take me into your studio? I promise I'll do any task you require.'

'You like my pictures? You think you understand them?' asked Sun doubtfully.

'Yes, yes. I was fortunate to have seen a few of them in my master's collections. The one I like most is the "Peonies in the Wind". I believe no one else could present that state of stillness and peace at the heart of the dancing peonies as you did.' Long expressed his idea confidently.

Everyone praised Sun's famous peonies painting for the eye catching strokes of pink and white that showed the dynamics of the blossoms in the wind. Sun never explained his expression. As long as his admirers were contented with their own interpretations and were ready to pay a high price for the work, Sun was happy to let them think what they liked about it. Sun had never expected that it would be a dish washing lad who could share his feeling of the calmness of the peonies in the moving wind.

'So, you know the art of painting? May I know who that lucky art master was to have you as his apprentice before?' Sun would rather this youth was trained than was really talented.

'No, I didn't learn about paintings or arts. I learned what I know from observation. But I do sincerely wish to learn from you. I have no money but I will work very hard, learn humbly and serve you wholeheartedly.'

It happened every time Sun stopped by a big city that some young people would come to ask him to be their drawing master. But they came with valuable gifts and their wealthy or powerful parents. As a traveling artist, Sun always had a good excuse to supervise them only for just one or two lessons. Sun came from a poor family. Even though he had talent, it was a long and difficult path before he became famous. He was already forty before his drawings could reach the ears of the imperial family. Sun had never liked those rich arrogant youngsters. He had no serious interest to teach anyone who had neither talent nor passion. But now standing in front of him was a young man with talent and passion, and Sun still hesitated. He was jealous and he was scared that his fame and prestige achieved over all those years of hardship would soon be usurped by the new star.

Whether I teach him or not, he would become a real competitor one day for he is a genius. Sun was sure of that. But a gem will be no more than a stone if it remains unpolished and buried. *I will be the stone keeper.* Sun made a selfish decision.

'Young lad, I never take apprentices so there will be no exception for you.'

Long was disappointed but before he could beg again, Sun continued, 'But you could come with me and work as my assistant as we travel from province to province. I would not teach you or pay you. I give no comments and answer no questions. You wouldn't be able to draw on paper or draw for anyone without my permission.'

Long kept nodding while Sun was telling all the conditions. 'Yes, I would follow all your commands,' Long promised with delight.

Long was contended with just the opportunity to work for a great artist and to travel and see different places. He believed that he could learn from a great artist by just working for him and observing his work. He was also glad to leave the city and see the world. The only thing he would miss was the chance of, from a distance, occasionally seeing the girl.

They would be leaving in a day's time. Long would like to see the girl and tell her in person the promises he had made in his heart. He would like her know that he would be back and to draw them the portraits he owed her and her mother. He went to the mansion but finally he lacked the courage to knock on the door.

But I will be back, and back as a great artist in a few years' time. We will have the time in the future. This was Long's belief at the time.

Gavin knew of course that Long would regret thinking this way and that he would regret his decision.

Running through Gavin's mind were memories of all those things he had put aside.

'One day, we will take a month's vacation in southern France, or Italy or wherever you wish to go. We must visit the Yangtze gorges before everything is drowned by the dam construction. Perhaps we should go to learn ballroom dancing together. We can watch that movie next week. I will help to make that album'.

Gavin could recall many such promises he had made to his wife, some of which he hadn't even had time to tell her. *We will have the time.* That had been Gavin's belief also.

We never know at the time what the right decision is. Do our decisions determine our fate or does fate determine what decisions we will make?

Had it not been for the ringing of the alarm clock that brought him back to reality, Gavin would have stumbled on lost in these trains of thought. It's time to go. At this minute, nothing could be more important than picking up Zoe from school, giving her a big hug and listening to her chatter about her friends and school on their way home.

Now, Gavin cooked and ate with Zoe every evening. He took her to Disneyland[2] the first day it was opened. He read her the first draft of whatever it was that he had just finished every day.

No one can be sure how much time we have ahead of us.

---

[2] It refers to the Hong Kong Disneyland, opened in September, 2005.

3

Why did she have to die?

'Daddy, was Long in love with the girl? When would they meet again? . . .'

Zoe had been asking the same questions since Gavin had read the second chapter to her the night before. She was fascinated by love stories. How much did an eight year old know about love? Gavin wondered. When he was eight, his mind was taken up only by knights and dragons, robots and monsters. Was Sofia like Zoe when she was her age? Gavin couldn't help relating things to his dead wife. She was always in his mind but recently he thought of her even more while he was working on this story.

'. . . . But I know, finally they will be happily ever after . . . .' Zoe was always optimistic. Who isn't when a fairy tale is being expected?

'We will see. Are you ready for tonight's chapter?' Actually Gavin was not quite sure if he was ready to disappoint Zoe.

'Yes, of course.'

For four years, Long followed Sun and didn't return to Nanjing. They travelled westward, up the Yangtze River to as far as the Chong Qing sub-prefecture in the Sichuan area before they turned back . . . .

Gavin opened another window on the laptop which showed a China Map. 'Here's Nanjing. It's situated on the vast plain of the lower reaches of the Yangtze River. Chong Qing is in central China, about midway up the Yangtze River.' Gavin traced along the Yangtze River to show Zoe the route. He had promised Sofia to go there with her. Now he could only imagine her companionship when he did the research.

Zoe kept nodding even though she was still in the mist. She was just a primary three student in an English medium school. Chinese geography and history were as remote to her as the ocean was to a frog but she knew that it was better not to say anything. Otherwise, her daddy might give her a lecture on China instead of going on with the story. She just kept nodding and responding with the affirmative 'Erhhhhh . . . Mmmmm'

Of course, Gavin could tell that Zoe was not interested at all or she would have endless questions on the topics. 'Okay, let's continue.' He returned to the page they'd been on.

. . . The new experience and the beauty of the nature in the river, its gorges and the mountains, had given Long much inspiration to draw.

Sun drew a lot as well. As he had decided, he never taught Long or gave him any comment on his drawings. He just drew as he normally did, neither giving emphasis to any technique, nor deliberately concealing anything. Long was requested to stand by his side attending his needs. Grinding the various ink slabs to give the optimum concentration of ink for different moods and styles. Fetching the different paintbrushes to match the desired strokes and images. Long observed and remembered every detail. As he had promised, he never drew on paper or asked any question. He practised in his old way with water on the table or the floor. He let pictures fade after pictures without catching the eye of anyone else. Long learnt Sun's skills to refine his own but he never attempted to imitate Sun's style. Over the years, Long had mastered and extended Sun's skills without relying on specific kind of paintbrushes or ink.

For the first two years, Sun and Long maintained a quiet and courteous relationship. Occasionally, they would have some casual talk but neither was keen to ask or learn more than what the other had said. One was too proud; the other felt inferior. Still, with time, a kind of understanding was built between the master and the apprentice.

When they stopped in the big cities and were surrounded by flattering admirers, Sun was sociable but, he was still an egocentric and conceited art master. Long could also see peace and gentleness under Sun's arrogance and indifference. That was when Sun was focused on his paintings or immersed in the beauty of the mountains and waters as they travelled.

'After my wife's death, I couldn't draw anymore until one day I rediscovered my inspiration when I sailed along the Yangtze River. Then I knew she was still there, everywhere, just not in the cities which she never liked.'

'If my paintbrushes could talk, they would tell you how much they hate to stay in the big cities. There, they have to give way to wine and feasts. My wife would have felt the same but it was just a few years' time that she could share the fruit of my success. Me, how could I hate them? Without maintaining and extending the social connections, inspiration alone wouldn't have kept my fame.'

Though Sun was greatly concerned with reputation and was proud to mention his painting hung in the Royal Palace, Long knew that it wasn't his most valuable masterpiece. His most treasured picture was hung in his room on the boat. It was the first portrait he had drawn for his wife in their poor old days.

Sun had mentioned once, 'The highest value of a picture is that it captures what I see and how I feel at the moment. It carries my memory. When the impression gets blurred in mind, it remains on the paper.'

Sun drew to remember but Long remembered in order to draw. 'I never have the chance to draw right at the moment so I have to remember and recall it in order to draw later when I get back to my "paper". I have not been able to keep a picture on paper but then every image is kept in my mind.'

Before hearing Sun's view, Long had never realized that people might forget. He could still remember every detail of his mother, of the lady and the girl. The girl, her image came to his mind all the time but would she have forgotten how he looked?

Before reflecting on Long's perspective, Sun had never thought of someone drawing for no purpose, neither for fame nor money, not even for the sake of memory. Long was satisfied just to draw. Sun had expected Long's heart to be filled with ambition as his own was when he was Long's age. But actually it was occupied by a girl whose name he had never asked.

'I hadn't had the courage to tell her how much I love her. I believed that a house servant didn't deserve her love but a great artist would. That's why I wished to become a famous painter. I didn't know that I would miss her so much but I do. Every mountain and valley I see, I wish she were by my side to share this beauty.'

Sun could feel how anxious Long was to see his girl again to tell her what he hadn't said years before. Besides, Sun had received letters recently from his friends in Nanjing, passing the message from the mayor to ask for his favour. So perhaps it was time that Sun should make the journey back.

When Sun and Long were getting near to the capital, they had already heard about artists from all over the country rushing into the city, to compete for a task that would be richly rewarded by the mayor. Once they stepped through the city gate, Sun was warmly received by his admirer, Master Li, Long's former master, who told him the whole story.

'The mayor is worrying about the deteriorating health of his only daughter. She has been mourning over her mother's death for over three years. Since then, no one has ever seen her smiling face or actually seen her face at all. The mayor told me that a few months ago, she grew more desperate and got very ill. It was because she felt that she couldn't stop her dead mother's image from fading out of her mind. She was afraid that one day she would lose her mother totally if she couldn't even recall her face. Poor girl! The mother and daughter had been much attached to each other.' Li took a long sigh before he could continue.

'The mayor was ready to offer a large reward for someone who could draw a portrait of his dead wife to cheer his daughter up again. The competition had attracted many artists but so far none of them could satisfy the girl. Who could draw according to just the girl's verbal description? I have told the mayor that besides you, the great Master Sun, no one else could achieve it. You are now the mayor's final hope.'

Sun was glad to be honoured as the greatest artist but he knew that flattery would not help him to achieve the task. He was confident to outdraw anybody with the most beautiful portrait of the lady if she was sitting in front of him but to draw according to someone's memory and description was an impossible task even for him. Sun knew that a drawing which would satisfy the mayor and his daughter could adorn his reputation but he had decided not to take the risk of losing to somebody who might have seen the lady before. Finally, it was only out of courtesy and curiosity that he agreed to go and checked out the competition.

Long followed Sun to the mayor's mansion. It was that big mansion, outside which Long had met that pale noble lady and her girl, the girl that he kept thinking of on his journey. Actually, when Long had overheard Li telling Sun about the case, he had suspected that Li was talking about her. Long had just refused to think in that way. But now, however sad it was, he had to face the reality. His heart was beating faster and faster as he approached the hall. He was sure it was that girl he loved and that her mother had died. But to his disappointment, he didn't see the girl he had so longed to see. She was staying behind a screen at the far end of the hall, describing her mum's face to the artists. He didn't know if she could recognize him as the attendant standing beside Master Sun.

Long followed the girl's descriptions and in his mind, he outlined the face and then filled it with all the details accordingly. In fact, he could still remember the lady's face and also that of the girl who he assumed was now hidden behind the screen. He had promised to draw them their portraits but he had never thought of having had to draw them from his memory.

Meanwhile, all the painters were attempting to draw what the perfect beauty should be in the eyes of a daughter but no two of their pictures looked even similar. 'Her face was as gentle as the moon . . . . she had the smile of the winter sun . . . .' There were no concrete details or scales to follow in the girl's description.

'Unless someone has met the lady before and can remember her face' wondered Sun. 'but if there was such an artist, he should have tried it already . . .'

One after another, the portraits were rejected. Some artists left. Some insisted and more came to make their attempts. Again and again, the girl repeated the description in her weakening voice, draining her mind for better wordings to present the image.

Long would like to stop her torture and disappointment at once. He knew that he was the only person who could recall the face of the lady as well as being able to present it accurately in a portrait. He was ready to break his promise and draw on a paper but he would not let himself surpass Sun openly.

'Sorry, I don't think I will be able to help . . . .'

Long was relaxed now to hear Sun's reply to the mayor. He would tell the whole story to Sun later and beg for his permission to draw on a piece of paper.

' . . . I believe that no artist would be able to restore the life of the beloved on paper.' Sun couldn't bear to witness the girl's disappointment anymore so he proclaimed his position authoritatively to end the business.

'Just give up the idea and let her rest.' This was Sun's last advice to the mayor before they left.

On leaving, Sun noticed that Long kept turning back. He was afraid that Long was tempted to build his fame with such selfish trials so he repeated his belief to Long, 'Just give up the idea and let her rest.'

That statement kept whirling in Long's mind. He understood what Sun meant. What the girl needed was not a portrait to linger on but the courage to get past the grief and leave it behind. Long didn't mention to Sun about his encounter with the girl and her mother and his promise to them for he didn't think it was necessary anymore. He didn't ask for paper to draw on. However, he did draw a portrait of the lady. He drew it on the handkerchief that the girl had given him.

Long didn't even dare to go near the mansion. He thought there was nothing he could do to help the girl. The best thing would be to leave her in peace.

Some days passed and one day Sun accidentally saw Long's portrait on the handkerchief. Long then told Sun everything, including his gratitude and feeling for the lady and the girl. Sun could see now why no one so far had been able to match the girl's mental image.

'You are the dumbest person I have ever met, not because you didn't produce the portrait to gain the money or fame. In that case, even though you would have shown yourself to be smart, I would still despise you. But you're so stupid in thinking that you couldn't help.' Sun scolded Long for the first time, like a father to a son.

'Look at your picture. I could see not just beauty but love, appreciation and respect, the feeling which the girl was expecting someone to share. It was obvious that the mayor couldn't share his daughter's loss because he hadn't observed the virtues of his wife in the way you two did. The girl was sad not because she felt others forgetting her mum's appearance but she felt lonely to find no one sharing her loss.'

Without waiting a moment longer, Long rushed to the mayor's mansion with the handkerchief. The door attendants were sad but seeing the portrait on the handkerchief, they let him in immediately. He got the same reaction from everyone on his way to the girl's room. The doctors were leaving, shaking their heads on their way out.

The girl was lying on her bed but no one, not even the mayor, stopped Long from going to her bedside. She was keeping her eyes opened with great effort and she was surprised to see Long.

'It was you! . . .' she took a long pause to breathe.

'Was it a dream? . . . I thought that time I had seen you among the painters . . . . but it had to be a dream . . . . If that was you, you would have drawn the picture for me.'

'Here's the picture.' Long opened the handkerchief and placed it in her hands. 'I am sorry to keep you waiting.'

A smile came across the girl's face for the first time since her mother had died. Her once rosy cheeks were now pale. It was true her bones showed through but the dimples were deep as they had always been in Long's memory.

This was the girl's last smile and it would be ever inscribed on Long's memory.

Gavin stopped here. Slowly, he closed the file and logged off while looking at Zoe to wait for her response. She had never been so quiet after story reading but that was because Gavin had never told her a sad story before. He had never written a sad story before.

Finally, she asked doubtfully, 'Daddy, ... so the girl died? . . .'

Gavin nodded.

'Why did she have to die? I feel so sad for her and Long.'

'I knew you would be upset by it, sweetie. I am sorry.'

'Then, why did you have to make the story so sad?'

'Sweetie, it's just part of the whole story. It'll get better from this point. Long hasn't even had the magic feather yet and things can be changed with the magic.'

'O, I know, so with the magic, Long will make her live again and then they will live happily ever after, right?'

'Er, may . . . be . . . We'll see.'

'Why did she have to die? Why did you have to make the story so sad?'

The questions kept coming up in Gavin's mind.

When the story of 'Long and the Magic Feather' was first formed in his mind, it was just another fairy tale with a young painter getting a magic feather to help him in realizing his dreams. Like most stories, the protagonist had to lose something to get the magic power as compensation and at the end he would discover his preference to give up the magic power for what he had lost. It was supposed to be just another fairy tale.

However, once Gavin started writing it, it just turned out to be gloomier and sadder than he had expected. Gavin knew that he had been projecting too much of his own loss and remorse on Long. It was meant to be written for the children's magazine.

Gavin had thought of cutting out the whole of chapters two and three, sending Long on adventures to get the magic feather right after being helped by the girl and her mum. Then by the time he returned, he found that the girl had already died but he would be ready to trade her life for the magic feather. Yes, the story could be simpler but Gavin decided to leave it as it was. He decided that he was ready to face 'death' in fictional form.

Death had appeared romantic to him during his days of youth when it seemed so far away. Both his parents were still alive and all his grandparents had left the world before he knew them or knew what death was. As a medical student, he had dissected a corpse. He used to joke about the images of the death messengers in the 'The Seventh Seal'. Then all of a sudden, one of these messengers was already by the bedside of his wife. Since then, death was something Gavin had avoided mentioning in his story and in real life. In talking about Sofia, he didn't even use the words, 'passed away'. He told Zoe that her mum had gone to the Fairyland and got lost there. It took some time for people who came to know him after his wife 'had left' to discover that she had gone forever.

'Why did she have to die?'

Gavin would like to ask the same questions if there had been someone writing his story. He knew that death could be just part of the process and not the end, just as it was for a prince to demonstrate his love, or for Mother Goat to show her wit. Gavin was not sure why Sofia had to die. Was it to make him a writer, to make him treasure Zoe, to make him face death? The only thing he was sure of was that his life would not be a fairy tale. Sofia would not find her way out of the Fairyland as Snow White was rescued through a kiss or the six little goats getting out alive from the wolf's tummy.

'Why did she have to die?'

Gavin knew it would take him some time to find out the answer but for the first time in four years, he thought he was ready to face death, to face his loss and remorse.

4

Do you think there are real fairies?

Long could have easily established his career when everyone was amazed by his portrait of the mayor's dead wife. Sun would be proud to crown Long as his successor or in other words to crown himself as the mentor of this bright young apprentice. For one reason, Sun had no choice for when the news spread, people would rush to be the first to claim support for the prodigy. For another reason, Sun had really grown fond of this young man throughout the years they'd travelled together. If one day someone would have to take his place, he would rather it was Long. But when Long expressed his wish to leave the city, Sun gave him the same support and trust he would have given to his own son if he had had one. He gave him the money he needed and loaded his luggage with the warmest clothes, all types of paint brushes, the best ink and the finest paper. Sun believed that inspiration would ignite Long's spirit again. Long just needed the time and space Sun had needed after his wife's death.

Months had passed since the death of the girl. Long was back upstream on the Yangtze River. He followed the route he had gone through with Sun. It was as if he didn't know anywhere else to go. He passed through the breathtaking scenery again, recalling the wish he had made last time. *I wish I would be back with my family.* He just had not expected that he would be back so soon and all alone.

Long didn't stop at any city. He was not aiming for any destination. He didn't know what he was running away from but he just felt the urge to move on. Last time, he and Sun came as far as Chong Qing. This time he kept moving further and further inland. No more villages, no more houses, no more people, and finally no more paths. Leaving his money behind, his luggage behind and his drawing tools behind, finally he just went on with his memory. When Long started off his journey, he just wanted to leave the city. Now as he went further and further, he was captivated by the beauty of nature. That was what made him move onward.

One day, he came to a lake to refill his water bottle. The water was so clear and blue. It was so quiet and calm as if the whole world were still and as if he was the only one moving on for no reason. He let himself sit down and he just sat there for hours, fascinated by the different colours of the water from different depths and angles. Actually, the colours varied still further with the passage of time. Crystal blue, cyan, turquoise, jade, green, ripened wheat, chrome yellow, orange, red, crimson, purple, violet, sapphire and then inky dark. Then twinkling here and there, stars appeared and finally sprinkled over the whole lake surface as if the whole sky was in its embrace. But when he looked up, he was surprised by the vast sea of stars that actually stretched out to no end. Then at eye level were the sparkles from the eyes of animals in the woods and fireflies dancing around. Night had fallen so quietly but darkness hadn't lessened life's magic. If there was really a fairy world then he thought he had found it. If the spirits could choose where to go, that would be the place, so peaceful and yet so lively. Long let himself lie down and closed his eyes. His spirit was high in the sky and his heart was open again.

'Wake up, young man! Wake up! Where are you from?'

Long opened his eyes and the first thing he saw was a pair of round eyes staring straight into his. He could feel a breath of warm air blowing onto his face. Looking sideways from the big round eyes, he could see golden hair reflecting in the sun.

'Ah! . . . .' Long drew a quick breath and sprang up as quickly as he could when he discovered that the round eyes belonged to a small hairy animal which had jumped on him and leaned over to study his face. When Long had startled from his sleep, the animal had swiftly climbed up a nearby tree. It was a golden monkey, hiding behind some twigs and leaves, scared but still peeking at Long curiously.

After a deep gasp to recover from the shock, Long walked closer to the tree. 'I am sorry. I didn't mean to scare you.' Long extended his arms to the golden monkey to show his apology and friendliness.

'I . . . I thought you were . . . sp . . . speaking to me. I . . . I didn't ex . . . expect a mon . . . monkey could speak,' Long stammered. The golden monkey then jumped up and down, making sounds as if making objection to what Long had said.

' . . . No hard feelings . . . I think I was just dreaming,' Long went on. He then burst out laughing when he realized how silly he had been, to try explaining to a monkey. It had been a long time since he'd heard his own voice and he found it ridiculous to be talking to a monkey. When Long laughed, the golden monkey made new sounds too as if it was laughing also.

The golden monkey climbed down and moved close to Long's legs. Long lifted it up and patted it gently on the back. Soon, the golden monkey started brushing Long's arms and then his face gently with its long bushy tail also. It seemed very excited and kept making noises as if it was talking to Long. Long felt much more relaxed now and then he really felt the animal was speaking to him, 'Welcome to our place. What's your name?'

'I am Long . . . . Are you really talking to me? Is this an illusion?'

Long began to feel scared again, not of the animal but of himself. He had to sit down to calm himself down. He must have gone crazy after being isolated from people for such a long time. The monkey kept making noises in different tones. Long observed and he was sure it was just trying to communicate in its own language. He didn't know what it was saying now. Long strained to listen for a long time and then when he got relaxed again, he discovered that he could understand what the golden monkey was saying through her own sounds.

'So, you can understand me also?' Long asked tentatively.

When he no longer felt self-conscious about the ridiculous idea that he was talking to a member of another species, he could finally make out what the monkey was saying. 'Yes and we can talk with other animals also. We make different sounds but we can understand each other if we pay attention and listen.'

Soon, Long and the golden monkey began communicating to one another as if language was no more a barrier. Then there came even interruptions from the birds flying by from time to time.

'Kit Kit's the chatterbox. Don't talk to her. Once she starts, she won't stop!' It was the jay who was insisting.

'Ask her to show you around. She knows everyone here,' the magpie offered.

'Let's have some breakfast first. I am very hungry,' suggested Kit Kit, the golden monkey.

'Good idea! I'm hungry, too. I haven't eaten anything for two days,' Long chimed in so naturally now as if he was just talking to a human friend.

After sharing some fruit for breakfast, Kit Kit began to show Long around. There were lakes, plateaus, ravines, hills, waterfalls and limestone pools but traces of other humans. 'So, no people live here?'

'Depending on what you mean by "here". There is a small population of the Tibetan tribe, living on the other side of that hill. They seldom come over to this side. They are contented with what they have and they only wish to preserve the tranquility here with its every single rock and leaf for the gods and for the goddesses.'

'So it's really a world for the fairies! Do you think they will mind if I stay here?'

'The tribe?'

'No, I mean the fairies or the gods and goddesses.'

'I don't think there should be a problem. Our ancestors have been living here for centuries. My friends and I are all living in peace. We are part of nature and I don't see why you cannot be part of it.'

Before sunset, Long, with Kit Kit on his shoulders, or sometimes ahead of him for a few steps to show the way, had covered a lot of ground and been through many different landscapes. Finally, they went into a jungle of arrow bamboo.

'Let's give Ding Ding and Dong Dong a surprise! They are my best friends'

But it was Long who got a surprise to find that Kit Kit's best friends were not golden monkeys but a panda couple. Soon they became Long's best friends too. They didn't make much noise but Long could understand them from their gestures as well. They taught Long to make a comfortable den with some fallen bamboo leaves and they shared their favourite dish with Long. Long tried the bamboo leaves but he preferred the fruits of the forest and the bamboo shoots.

"Long settled down living happily with his new friends."

It was in this way, Long settled down in the arrow bamboo jungle, living happily with his new friends. He observed and respected the harmony of life in nature and soon he could call every single animal in the area by his or her name. During the cold winter nights, he slept with the pandas, nesting in a big hollow tree. On the hot summer days, he bathed with the golden monkeys in the cool water of the colourful limestone pools. He didn't know how long he had been staying there for as he had no plan to leave, it didn't really matter to count the days.

When Gavin mentioned the colourful limestone pools, the observant Zoe was already following his gaze up to the photo on the shelf top. It was the picture of her mum on the slope with those limestone pools behind her. 'Did you see golden monkeys in those pools?' Zoe asked seriously.

'Uh . . . no, . . .' Gavin hadn't expected the distraction but he realized immediately that he was the one being distracted first. Taking an album down from the bookshelf, he continued to explain, 'we didn't see any golden monkeys but they are supposed to be an endangered species, in Jiuzhaigou, in the province of Sichuan.

'And so are the pandas?'

'Yes, we didn't see any of them either.' He showed the album to Zoe and continued, 'But we saw all those waterfalls, colourful lakes and pools. It's really peaceful there.'

'You looked so young at that time.' Zoe looked at the pictures and then turned back to look up at Gavin who was now holding her on his lap.

'Yes, of course, that was twelve years ago when we went for our honeymoon.'

'It's beautiful. Is it real?'

Gavin nodded as he kept scanning the pictures, page by page, gently touching the face of Sofia in the pictures as if she were really there.

'I didn't know that there was a fairy world in China.' Zoe was puzzled.

'When I was young I never expected to find one either. It was your mum who showed me. Just like you, your mum loved fairy tales so I promised her we would go to Europe for our honeymoon. I was thinking of the Neuschwanstein Castle in Germany, castles along the Rhine, the Lake District in England, the Alps, Denmark—fairy tale kingdom, and . . . but she suggested Jiuzhaigou so we could save money. Besides, I didn't have a long holiday.'

'Do you think there are real fairies there?'

'There are a lot of legends in Jiuzhaigou. Almost every lake has its own love story which usually ends with the couple or the girl becoming fairies.'

'But mummy is not there?'

'No, or she would have known her way back. Remember I told you that she was lost in Fairyland where no people had been before. Or at least, no one can come back from there to tell us where it is. It is an endless field blanketed with all sorts of flowers in every shade of every colour. The fairies live among the flowers and . . . .'

' . . . unless they want to show themselves, you can never distinguish a fairy from a tiny insect.' It was Gavin's first published tale and Zoe had read it many times that she knew the lines well.

'But if Periwinkle could help Princess Mariana to find the way out, she would be ready to help mummy, right?'

'. . . Yes, ... if your mummy met Periwinkle . . . .' Gavin hesitated but still he repeated the same fantasy with such ease.

Gavin thought he was ready to face the truth of death and was determined to tell Zoe, 'your mummy won't come back because she was not in Fairyland. She has actually died.' While he was still struggling whether to tell her or not, the phone rang. He was glad that it rang so finally, he didn't have to decide. He needed more time and there would be time.

Gavin went to pick up the phone and left the room as he answered it. He gestured Zoe to sleep but once he turned his back, Zoe went back to reading the story.

Every morning, Long woke up as the first stream of light from the horizon crept quietly among the dense bamboo and swept across his face. This morning, just like any other morning, Long woke up and the first thing he did was to greet the early birds. He could hear a newcomer among the morning choir. The voice was outstanding and sweet. Long followed the sound and was astonished to spot a colourful bird flying swiftly and merrily among the bamboo. It was bigger than the average bird with a long ribbon-like tail. Long tried to ask her name. The bird wouldn't say but flew away gracefully.

In the days that followed, the bird kept coming around. The other animals began to talk about her.

'Her voice is so sweet. That could only be coming from heaven,' chirped the canary.

'Look at her feathers. They glitter under the sun and glow at night,' exclaimed the butterfly.

'She is definitely a phoenix,' declared the old tortoise, 'I saw one two hundred years ago.'

'She might be still a baby,' guessed Dong Dong, the female panda.

'You are welcome to join us,' Long called out every time when he was sharing fruits and nuts with the others.

Day after day, she came closer and closer. And after some days, she would even fly down and sing for a short while on Long's shoulder. She enjoyed Kit Kit's jokes and her laughter was like bells so Kit Kit called her Ling Ling.

Then one day, she disappeared. Two days had passed. Long missed her. Three days had passed. Long started to worry about her and so did the other animals. Instead of their usual routines to play hide and seek or bathe in the lakes, they agreed to go and look for Ling Ling.

Zoe was wondering what had happened to Ling Ling. She was so eager to read on but Gavin was back leaning in the doorway. He was still on the phone but he knew he needed to show his presence to get Zoe to go to sleep.

'. . . .' Listening to the phone, Gavin was at the same time shaking his head and pointing his watch to notify Zoe that it was really late. He remained at the doorway, however.

'No, I have told Kate that I'm not coming.' Gavin tried to speak softly.

'. . . .'

'I know but it's in Shanghai . . . .'

'. . . .'

Still talking on the phone, he gestured Zoe to close the laptop and go to bed at once.

'. . . You know, I don't want to leave on the weekend . . . . I have a workshop.'

'. . . .'

'No, my parents will be out of town.'

'. . . .'

'I'll see. I'll call you back . . . . Now it's my time for Zoe, . . .' Gavin was getting impatient with the phone and with Zoe who just ignored him and was still reading.

'. . . .'

' . . . . Okay, okay, bye . . . I'm hanging up. I'll call you later.'

Once Gavin was with her, Zoe turned off the laptop and dived under the blanket, 'Goodnight daddy.' She knew that if she behaved well, she could bargain for a longer story reading on Friday night, and that would be just the next night.

'Goodnight sweetie. Fly to Fairyland in your dream.'

5

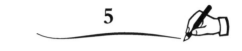

If it is heaven's will . . .

. . . they agreed to go and look for Ling Ling.

What happened was that as Ling Ling had not been as vigilant as before, she'd flown further and further. She'd flown to the other side of the hill and was spotted by the hunters there. Those Tibetan villagers never hunt further than their territory but they believed that whatever found in their areas must be approved by Mother Nature and the heavenly gods for their consumption. One day, the villagers saw this beautiful bird flying and singing above their fields.

'Look, it's a phoenix!'

'It's the legendary bird from the heavenly kingdom.'

'It must be a gift from heaven that she comes here to bring us fortune.'

'Let's catch the bird.'

And they did. They set a trap and caught this rare animal easily as she came down to eat the seeds in the trap, thinking that all creatures were kind and friendly. They put the phoenix in an ornamented cage, in the centre of the temple.

'We shall keep it in our temple so we can worship it.'

When Long and the bigger animals began their search for Ling Ling, some flying insects had headed off to the other side of the hill. They returned with the news they had heard from their friends on the other side.

'The tribesmen have caught a beautiful bird. It was . . .' the enthusiastic cicada couldn't wait to report all the details.

Big brother mantis gestured him to take a break and ended the report with the most up-to-date news, 'A special ceremony will be held tonight to crown it as the holy bird of the tribe.'

'It must be Ling Ling. Let's go and rescue her,' suggested Kit Kit.

'It's too risky. They may catch us as well,' cried Timi, the rabbit.

'Would they dare? I can roar and threaten to eat them. All humans are scared of me,' boasted the tiger Nam. He took a glance at Long, remembering his promise to him when he was welcomed by Long to become one of his friends, so he added, 'except Long of course.'

'I will go by myself,' said Long. 'They will not hunt a man.'

'But if they capture you or try to hurt you, you are not strong enough to fight back by yourself,' said Ding Ding.

'We don't fight to solve problem. We can talk,' Long said decisively.

'We can talk also so we will go with you,' volunteered the other animals.

Long could understand their concern so he didn't argue. After he made them promise to remain peaceful and listen to him, he let them go along with him.

The tribesmen were friendly towards Long. For one reason, they seldom had any visitors and they were overjoyed to have a guest especially on this great day. Secondly, they were shocked to see this man being followed by a whole gang of animals, small and large, mild and fierce. They believed that he must be special. Considering Long as an honourable guest, the chief received him warmly at the temple. Long asked the other animals to wait outside the temple and they obeyed and remained seated.

The holy bird had remained in silence since the moment she had been caught but once she saw Long stepping into the temple, she called out to him. Following the distinctive voice, Long looked up and saw Ling Ling in the cage. The chief followed Long's glance and was proud to introduce Long to their holy bird. Long told the chief frankly that he had come to ask for the release of the bird.

'It's disrespectful not to accept the sacred gift of heaven,' the chief refused politely.

Long did not want to anger or disappoint the tribe so he agreed. 'Indeed, this is your holy bird. It must be sent from heaven to look after your land and bring blessings to it.'

He looked around at the statues and paintings of other gods in the temple. Then he continued, 'and so are all these gods, I believe.'

'Yes, that's why we always worship them in the temple,' replied the chief.

'But these are statues. You don't keep the gods themselves in the temple?' asked Long.

'Of course,' puzzled the chief.

'Then why do you have to keep the holy bird in a cage? Is it not supposed to fly over other places and bring blessings to other people as well?'

Noises arose from corners to corners as the villagers began whispering and sharing their views. The tribesmen were not selfish people and neither was the chief. Finally, he agreed to release the bird but he still had some doubts. He was doubtful about whom this young man was. How does he know about the bird and how is it the bird seems to know him? Why do all the other animals obey him? Is he sent by heaven?

The chief decided to test Long's patience and power. 'Our craftsman died last month so we may need to keep the bird longer until we can find someone to make a good statue.'

Long had no idea of the chief's intention, he just wanted to save Ling Ling. He knew well what he could do so he asked for a scroll of paper, some ink and a paintbrush.

Without even looking at the bird, Long drew at his leisure. Everyone in the temple was captivated by the speed and confidence he showed in the drawing. When the picture was held up after less than a minute, the people were all amazed to see their holy bird so presented with such vivacity on the paper as if it was about to fly out among them.

The chief knelt immediately before Long, followed by all his tribesmen to plead for mercy. 'Your Holiness, please pardon us for our foolishness in catching the holy bird and challenging your power.' The tribe was deeply convinced that Long was a god or at least a messenger from heaven.

Ling Ling was released and at once, she flew to Long's shoulder. Long didn't want to cause any more suspicion so he said nothing. He let the people believe in what they believed and he went back to the bamboo jungle with the animals.

"They could see another colourful bird hovering in the air."

One the way back, they could see another colourful bird hovering in the air. She was much bigger than Ling Ling and looked more like a phoenix, the image of which he had seen before in pictures. Ling Ling was very nervous as she told the others that the bigger bird was her mum. She bade farewell and flew back to her mum before the latter came down.

Life returned to normal, only that now they had one more pastime. Realizing that Long could draw his friends always urged him to do so. Long drew on the ground with any twig or branch he could pick. Sometimes he drew portraits of the animals to amuse them and at other times, he let them have a scavenger hunt of the things he drew. Whatever he drew, the animals who were playing would have to find it from the surroundings. Long would always draw them something that would be difficult but not impossible to find.

Occasionally, they would miss Ling Ling's companionship and her beautiful voice but they could see it was right that she should be safe with her mum.

One day, Long heard the long missed voice again. No, it was not one but two voices. Not long after he heard them, he could spot his friend, Ling Ling flying down to him. She had grown a bit bigger and following her was that phoenix which had accompanied Ling Ling away a few months before. Ling Ling landed on Long's shoulder but she was now a bit heavier. The bigger phoenix landed in front of Long and in an instant, she had transformed into a beautiful lady in colourful clothes.

'Don't be afraid. I am the Goddess Phoenix . . .' She pointed to Ling Ling and continued, 'and this little friend of yours is my willful daughter. She is just a baby chick so she can't do any magic yet. She has told me everything. She was so curious about life on earth that she had secretly slipped out of the heavenly gate last time when you saw her. Her disobedience had brought her the dangers of which you know but she should have learnt her lesson by now. Thank you for saving her. In fact, those people should thank you also since I was already on my way to find her. If I had seen her in a cage, I likely would have ruined the whole village in anger. Anyway, thank you very much.'

'Don't mention it. We're happy to have met Ling Ling, I mean your daughter. Can she come again if she wishes?'

'No, we aren't supposed to come without the Jade Emperor's permission. In fact, she's been punished and held in custody for three months. This time, we'd asked His Majesty to let us come to show our gratitude. I'd like to thank you with a gift. What would you like to have?'

In a blink, rocks and trees in front of him were turned into heaps of gold, jewelry and a grand house, one after another. Each time, Long just shook his head.

'I appreciate your nice offer very much but I really don't need anything. I have my friends here, I enjoy my time. I've had all the good things and I feel contented with a simple life.'

The lady was very pleased with Long's integrity. She took out a feather from under her sleeve and put it in Long's hand. 'I insist that you keep this. It's just one of my feathers. I've picked it out and I can't put it back. It is nothing but a feather . . . unless it is the will of heaven for you to be its master.'

Long didn't know what it meant to be its master or what heaven's will was but he knew he couldn't refuse anymore so he took it.

After reviewing what he had written so far, Gavin was ready to continue. It was Friday and he had to work harder because he had to attend the regular editorial meeting in the afternoon. He should have enough to read to Zoe for that night but he would like to finish the whole story since he wouldn't work on Saturday. He was planning to take Zoe to the movies this weekend and then perhaps go ice-skating. Zoe liked this sport and she could do it well. He'd tried but he couldn't really stand up. He was not confident with any sport that required balancing, be it roller-skating, ice-skating, cycling, skateboarding, or just walking on a narrow ledge. *Is it really Heaven's will that we possess or do not possess some talent? . . . . Hey, focus, why am I thinking about balancing now?*

Written by...

Gavin returned to the computer and his fingers danced on the keyboard as he already had in mind what he wanted to say.

Long continued to have pleasant times with the other animals. He put the feather in his sleeve and occasionally, he would take it out to appreciate its beauty. Soon he discovered that the colours of the feather were changing all the time. One day, when he was sitting by the lake, observing the colours of the feather, Kit Kit asked him to have a scavenger hunt with him. There were no sticks of the proper size within reach so he just dipped the feather in the water and drew on the rock he was sitting on.

The moment Long finished drawing a bamboo shoot, a real one was seen in its place.

Long picked up the bamboo shoot and examined it with surprise. 'Hey, Kit Kit, you're quick this time. I didn't even see you taking it out or putting it here. How did you know beforehand that I was going to draw a bamboo shoot?' He was still looking at it and murmuring, 'And it's exactly of the same size.'

He looked up at Kit Kit since there was no response. Then he looked where he'd drawn and Long was shocked to see that his picture was completely gone. He was used to his pictures fading, but never this quickly. Kit Kit was too shocked to speak. She was staring at the bamboo shoot in Long's hand with an open mouth. 'I didn't get it. It . . . just . . . . just . . . appeared there.'

'What do you mean by it just appeared there?' puzzled Long.

'You . . . try . . . again. Draw something else.' Kit Kit wanted to prove her speculation.

Long drew a rock. A rock of exactly the same size and shape appeared. Long was shocked also. He tried something that couldn't be found in early winter. He drew a peach and it appeared. He drew something that couldn't be found in this place in any season. He drew a bowl of hot rice and it appeared, with steam coming out.

More animals had gathered around as they experimented. They were all shocked at first and overjoyed after a few trials to find that it was a magic feather.

Kit Kit asked for it to try. Though she could hold the feather and imitated Long's action, she could only scribble some lines. Some parts already dried up before she finished the rest. Nothing appeared.

Now Long remembered and understood what the Phoenix Goddess had said. He was meant to be the master of the magic feather. It was heaven's will for the feather to belong to someone with the talent and skill to draw even with water.

At first, Long was scared to use this magical power. But as the weather got colder and food was difficult to find, he was tempted to use it more and more often. They had survived the cold winters before but the convenience and abundance provided by the magical power just made the temptation irresistible. Long had thought of the limits but as he had no last wish, it didn't really matter if each time would be the last time. He was prepared that one day the feather would cease to be magical.

In the beginning, Long drew when they did not have enough to eat. Then he began to draw what they wished for, those juicy summer fruits they missed, raw meat for the predators and the food he liked, steamed buns, congee and dumplings. In the beginning, he drew himself a blanket to keep himself warm at night. Soon, he drew a big coat and then more clothes so he'd have changes and choices of what to wear. In the beginning, he drew some materials so to build a hut. Soon, he drew a bigger cottage and with more furniture added every day.

Spring came and went and summer came. Mother earth was once again providing enough of what the animals needed. One by one, they resumed their natural habits, eating from the trees and grazing over the fields. Long, however, was missing his civilized life. He was spending less and less time with the animals as he didn't need to find food with them. He was spending most of his time now thinking of city life.

Gavin had thought of a moral ending that Long's greed soon wore the feather out. He would be disappointed at first but then his friends would make him realize that he didn't need it. He would return to his friends and they lived happily ever after under the care of Mother Nature. That was his simple idea before he actually started writing and taking both Long and himself through the tortures of death and regret.

That night Zoe inspired him with the idea of a happy ending—the magic could bring the girl back to life and they would live happily ever after. Gavin liked that idea. That would be the only thing that would really make a happy ending. That should be what Long would wish for if he could do magic. So Gavin continued.

Long realized the feather had been used so many times that it had started to wear out. It might only last a few more pictures. Now he began to think seriously what last wishes he should satisfy. *To return to the capital. I can draw a horse and then a boat and enough money to spend on the way. I can buy a big mansion to hang my paintings in. Then rich people will come to appreciate them and invite me to draw for them. I will start my career and I will be one of the best known artists.* For many days and nights, while all his friends were enjoying their time under the sun or sleeping soundly, Long was struggling with his thoughts.

Are these the things I wish for? I could have had them without the magic feather if I hadn't escaped from them in the first place.

If it is heaven's will for me to own this magical power, it shouldn't be to bring me back to what I have abandoned. No, not after these many years.

I can't go back from here. But if I were destined to live that life I've already abandoned, then the only way will be to return to the time before I left it behind. Yes, yes. I believe I can establish my fame through my own talent. If I have the chance again.

But who is to share my success?

No, if I could go back in time, I should go back to before that. I should return to the time when it wasn't too late to draw her the portrait.

Finally, an idea flashed into Long's mind. If only he could draw a doorway that let him walk through to that mansion, back on the date he saw the girl again behind the screen . . . .'

With the idea in his mind, Long drew a simple doorway. It appeared before him. Long closed his eyes and in his mind he was thinking. *I am going back to that mansion . . .* and so it was Long stepped through the doorway he'd made and back to the time he remembered.

While Gavin was writing the paragraphs on Long's struggling thoughts, he himself was also struggling against his own fantasy.

If I had that magic feather, I could have a happy ending too. Could it possibly be heaven's will that I had become a fairy tale writer to borrow some magic? Long, can I borrow the feather I imagined for you?

An idea flashed into his mind or you may say Gavin was actually out of his mind in that flash of time. Instead of typing what you have read just now, he typed the last sentence as:

Long closed his eyes and in his mind, he was thinking. *I am going to my author and I will lend him the magic feather . . .* and so it was Long stepped through the doorway he'd made and . . .

6

I must have been crazy

Long, can I borrow the feather I imagined for you?

  Crazy! Gavin, what are you thinking of?

  Gavin scolded himself for being distracted by this crazy idea. He turned to the fridge behind him to get a can of cold Coke to clear his mind.

  But while he was doing so, Long was stepping across the doorway. He opened his eyes and saw himself in a room the like of which he had not known before. Right in front of him, there was a big desk with books and paper piling up. Behind the desk was . . . . the back of a chair? It seemed a comfortable one. It was turning and on it was this short haired man in strange checkered clothes. In his hand was a red cylinder that he had just taken out from an illuminated cupboard behind the chair. The man turned and had his face hidden behind a black square box now. Then all of a sudden, 'Pop'.

  'Ahhhhhh . . . .' screamed Gavin and Long simultaneously and the scream lasted for at least two more seconds as if they were now trying to scare each other.

  Long was scared by that unexpected 'pop' sound when Gavin opened the soda can and from which the 'tiny geyser' gushing out became even more severe when Gavin sprang up in fear.

Gavin was nervous when he sensed someone in his peripheral vision and he was genuinely scared when he looked up to see this long haired stranger in some outlandish gown, standing right in front of him. Gavin sprang up from his chair and backed up two steps, till his back was against the shelf, spilling more coke in the move.

Long backed up also and grasped the first thing he could reach. Though it was just a small rectangular box with a lot of buttons and symbols, Long felt more secure to have something in hand. At least he had something to throw to defend himself if necessary.

Each man remained frozen staring at the other. Finally Gavin broke the ice, 'Who are you?' He was not really interested to get a reply but he just asked to distract the stranger's attention while he was glancing around after his mobile phone. Each saw that object as a means of defence. Gavin had in mind that the man in front of him must be some insane intruder rather than a dangerous burglar.

'My name is Long,' Long answered plainly and he bowed naturally before he resumed his on—guard posture.

Gavin hadn't been paying attention but now he found himself repeating the name 'Long' in his mind. 'L-o-n-g, . . . my 'Long' . . .' Gavin wondered in disbelief. He looked at Long from head to toe and from toe to head again. Then he asked tentatively, 'where are you from?'

'I'm from Nanjing, the capital. That's where I was born, that's where I grew up. But it's a long time now since I've been there.' Long bowed again. After so many years not dealing with people, Long had never forgotten to respond politely.

'In the Ming Dynasty? In the reign of the Emperor Yongle?'

'Yes.' Long was puzzled. When else it could be?

'You came out from my story?' Gavin tried to ask as directly as he could. But he couldn't even convince himself with what he was saying.

Slowly, he moved a few steps towards Long and with both hands raised so as not to make Long feel threatened. When Long started moving a step back, Gavin stopped. Looking Long in the eyes, he took a deep breath and began to ask question after question, 'You are very good at drawing?'

Long nodded.

Gavin moved a step forward, 'Your mentor is called Sun?'

Long nodded.

Gavin took another step forward. 'You went to Jiuzhaigou?'

Long looked puzzled this time. But then Gavin was quick to realize that of course Long would not have heard of the name so he asked in another way. 'There, you met your friends, a golden monkey called Kit Kit and the pandas, Ding Ding and Dong Dong?'

Long nodded again.

Gavin came still closer. 'You got a magic feather from the Phoenix Goddess?'

As expected, Long nodded.

If light could be emitted from a person, Gavin would have been seen glowing brighter and brighter with every nod of Long's. He was now at arm's length from his character, ready to ask the last question he had in his mind. He cleared his throat and spoke carefully word by word. 'You drew a doorway and stepped through to here?'

Long nodded and before he could say what he was about to say, the overjoyed Gavin was already hugging him as if Long was an old friend. Long was shocked by Gavin's absurd move.

Though he had not received any formal Confucian education, he did know the proper courtesy of keeping a distance between acquaintances. And besides, they had not even met each other before. He pushed away from Gavin and declared in a firm though polite tone, 'I demand for your respect, mister. I don't know you at all. Would you please keep a distance from me?'

Gavin backed off in embarrassment. 'I'm sorry. I'm just overexcited.'

Finally, Long had the turn to say what he wanted to say, 'so you are that someone called "My Author"?'

Gavin nodded with a smile of pride. He pointed at himself, 'yes, me . . .' and then pointed to Long and continued, ' . . . . your creator . . .' But Gavin's proud moment couldn't last long; there was too much he didn't understand about the situation.

Now Long had to put his manners aside. He couldn't wait for Gavin to finish because he really had to get things clear. 'Just before I came here, I was still thinking of going back to the earlier time when I could have drawn a portrait for my friend. That would have saved her disappointment, the great disappointment from which she died. Then a strange idea came to my mind while I was stepping forward through the doorway. I don't know why but I was thinking of going to someone called "My Author" to lend him my magic feather. The next moment, I was here.'

Long was getting louder as he spoke. It was as if he couldn't hold his anger any more. 'I was here. I was supposed to go back and save a life and I was here, in this strange place, talking to a strange man, called "My Author".'

Gavin understood all that Long said. It was just that it didn't make sense. But it did. Long's expression told him that he had to answer, had to explain himself. 'That's not my name but my role. I am an author. My name is Gavin. I have created you and I have written whatever has happened to you up until now. And you stepped through this doorway because . . .' But Gavin couldn't finish that sentence because what he wanted to say wasn't quite true. He hadn't written Long through a doorway into this room . . . But before he could think further on this point, Long had resumed his aggressive stance.

'So you made her die?'

'Yes, . . . but . . . that's an event in the plot . . . .' Gavin could sense the anger in Long's voice, so he knew he had to cut straight to the point. 'I was going to make her live again. You know with that magic doorway, you could travel back in time to save her. But . . .'

' . . . but then you changed your mind and brought me here?'

'No, I didn't.' It was Gavin's reflex to defend himself but now he realized that he was denying the lie he'd almost told himself just a moment ago. And then on second thoughts, he had to admit the possibility. 'Maybe I did.' But I didn't know I was doing it, he thought to himself. Maybe . . .

Gavin turned and rushed back to the computer to check what he *had* written. 'Come and read my story. No, I mean, *your* story.'

Long followed cautiously, still holding his strange temporary weapon. He stopped just behind that black square thing on the table. Something on its other side had captivated this author man, so Long crept round to Gavin's side to see what it was. It was bright, a bright screen. It was a lighted background with all sorts of symbols at the edges. In the middle was a white background like a piece of paper full of words. Then as Gavin scrolled up and down the page, Long was surprised by the sight of words moving up and down in lines. After the initial amazement of the movable pages, Long's attention was drawn to the words themselves. It didn't take him long to realize that the words should be read horizontally from left to right. The next moment he was shocked to find from the few lines he was reading that the text before him described exactly what had happened to him a short while ago.

'You could control my thinking,' murmured Long.

'I really wrote what was in my mind,' murmured Gavin.

The men spoke almost at once. It was to express their shock rather than expecting any response from the other.

Both were reading over and over that last ridiculous sentence which seemed to have worked the magic.

'I can't believe that I had really written it in that way. I must have been crazy at that moment . . . ' Gavin was murmuring to himself in disbelief.

Then realizing that the magic did indeed work, he was eager to find someone to share his excitement. He turned to Long and grabbed his arm, imploring; he held it emotionally. 'Tell me that it's true. I'm not crazy. It must be heaven's will. I can bring my wife back. Can you believe it?' Gavin couldn't control his excitement.

But Long was unwilling to accept that he was only someone's character. *I can't believe it. I know I can't control my life but I have never thought of my fate being determined by another man.*

7

You have to believe in it

Gavin could feel the desperation in Long's voice. He could understand that feeling, the feeling of not being able to control one's own fate. When Gavin was young, he believed that he was the master of his own life. But as he grew older and looked backward, he knew that everything seemed to work out according to some blueprint, some plan to which he never had complete access.

In those happy years, he had not a single complaint but gratitude for the fact that things were so well worked out. If things had happened according to his own plan, he might never have met his wife or fallen in love with her. He would have pursued that girl who was studying pharmacy. He was thankful for this 'plan' beyond his control. Thanks to that plan, there came that day a broken cable caused a delay in the train traffic and he had to take the bus. He had never liked the bus because he could never tell how long he had to wait for it and he couldn't bear the unpredictable road traffic. But that day, on the bus he wouldn't have taken if he'd had the choice, he met Sofia. Sofia had never liked the MTR[3] since

---

[3]   Mass Transit Railway—it is a major public transport in Hong Kong, started off with the underground trains. It is with recent

she hated that feeling of being isolated from the world of fresh air and light.

The 'plan' worked well for Gavin until Sofia was diagnosed with cancer and died soon after. He could understand Long's disappointment and anger. But while the magic doorway brought Long to discover himself trapped within walls, it reopened Gavin's road to the belief that things happened for a purpose. Sofia's death made him choose the path to become a fairy tale writer. This path led him to experience a miracle that could only work through fairy tales. He would like to share his feeling with Long. He was going to have a long talk with his "old friend" but not now. At present, the most important thing was to bring his wife back.

Gavin tried to suppress his excitement about what he was going to do. He comforted his friend not without real concern but being a self-centred person, he wasn't considerate enough. 'You should feel glad that we have a chance to meet and you can talk to me directly. You know what? I'm your genie like in a story. Tell me your wishes. You can just tell me how you want your life to be and I can fulfill it . . . .'

Such an arrogant man! This was Long's first little impression of Gavin.

'In the meantime, it will be a good experience for you to see this world. You can stay here in this room, read your story, any other books, watch TV, have some snacks, drink some soda, wear my clothes, take a rest on my bed and do whatever you like. Be my guest and help yourself but just don't leave my house. I will bring back my wife. She'll be well again. That

---

development such as the opening of Airport and Disney lines and the incorporation of the KCR (Kowloon Canton Railway) and the light rail trains, that it is no longer just a subway system.

shouldn't take long. I will be back before Zoe comes home. I promised to make her spaghetti for dinner tonight. By the way, Zoe's my daughter, a very lovely girl. She knows about you. She will be very excited to meet you and her mum, of course. Then we can show you around this world and all its wonders before your return to your world to save the girl and live happily with her . . . happily ever after . . .' Gavin was too overwhelmed to notice that he was telling too much and talking too fast.

Long couldn't really follow his dancing mind especially when there were so many unfamiliar terms. He could only hear a lot of 'I' and 'my'. *Such a self-centred man!* This was Long's second little impression. But as his habit, he still tried to remember every word he heard by picturing everything as symbols.

' . . . You can still save the mayor's daughter girl but just a bit later because . . . I would like to borrow your magic feather to save my wife first.'

Although so far Long couldn't understand much of what Gavin had been saying, he did get this message. 'What do you plan to do with my feather?' asked Long, not caring for this man's intentions, and grasping tightly the feather inside his sleeve.

'To return to the time before my wife was diagnosed with cancer just as what I intended for you to do, to return to your first love before she died.' Gavin was confident with his plan now.

'What's cancer?'

'I have no time to explain. It's a terrible disease that will cause death if it cannot be detected early enough to get the right treatment . . .'

So this man's wife has died. Long could feel his loss.

Gradually Gavin's excitement died down as he was giving way to doubt now. The voice of that 'little guy' called Rationality was restructuring his thoughts. *What's the use of knowing it earlier? It cannot be prevented. An earlier detection might save her but it might as well prolong her fear, false hope and torture. Are you going back just to make yourself feel better by devoting more time to her this time around? Are you ready to live through the suffering with her one more time? Are you going to involve Zoe through the torturing process now when she could understand better? And wait, where would Zoe be if . . . ?* Gavin hated such moments of self-doubt.

While Gavin was struggling with his thoughts, Long was observing him in silence. This was the man who could control people's lives. But he wasn't a god, Long was sure of that. Long was jealous of this man's power, his power to create, to destroy, to decide how things would be. It was unfair. When Long saw tears in the corners of Gavin's eyes, he knew this man was as human as he was, powerless against his own fate. Long began to pity Gavin.

Gavin wouldn't let his thoughts buried under rationality. They wiggled through. *No, I don't just mean to be with her through the past again. I need Sofia now and in the future and with Zoe. I can't change the past but I will change the future. I have to bring her back from where she is now.* After all, it was fantasy that had helped Gavin lived through these years when rationality couldn't offer that comfort.

'I have to bring her back from the other world.' Gavin was determined as he secretly wiped the tears off the corner of his eyes in a quick move.

'The Infernal world? You mean Hell?' asked Long as if he was reading from Gavin's mind.

'No,' answered Gavin firmly. Not even the world of the death—for four years, he had denied the idea that she had died. 'Sofia is in Fairyland. I saw her there among the flowers and the flying seeds. She just got lost there. If you can come out here into this room from a story world then she should be able to come out also. I just need to go to that world and find her.'

Long was initially confused but on giving the idea a second thought he was inclined to agree with Gavin's logic. It seemed that this man's wife was also in a story world like his but at the same time she was real. Perhaps there were many worlds, all equally real. Perhaps it was possible to visit these many worlds if one had the right magic. Long's head was spinning with questions as to what was real and what wasn't, what could be real and what couldn't.

And while Long's head span, Gavin fetched down a book from the bookshelf. He turned the pages and showed Long a colourful full-page illustration of the Fairyland where his wife was. It was a vast field with wildflowers of all different colours. In the distance were rows of silhouetted trees. The sky was blue dissolving into pastel lilac, with a soft spiraling ray of light coming from above. Flying over the flower field were dandelion pappus and seeds of other kinds, butterflies, ladybugs, fireflies, dragonflies and with them, not much larger, flew the humming birds. Sitting among the flowers or flying among the insects were the tiny fairies roughly the size of bumble bees. Each of them had a pair of translucent silky wings on the back and a colourful dress resembling the petals of different kinds of flowers.

'That's beautiful!' Long exclaimed with appreciation for the water colour picture so different in style from what he was used to.

'That's beautiful!' Gavin exclaimed with the image of the actual scene in his mind.

As Long was admiring the colours and peacefulness presented in the picture, he was also contrasting it with what he knew of the Chinese Infernal World for the dead souls. It was dark with an ever burning hell fire. The wicked souls would stay there forever, undergoing the torturing punishments appropriate to their sins. He was certain that his mother, the noble lady and her daughter could go through the judgment of the Infernal Emperor, and emerge in the world again. But picturing them going through such a place of trial, still hurt. Long could picture his loved ones being guarded by the hell guards with ox heads and horse faces, conducted on the path to reincarnation. On the way they would cross a bridge guarded by an old woman. They had to drink the bowl of tea offered by her so to forget everything in their previous lives. In contrast to this terrible scene, Long was so touched by the Fairyland Gavin had created for his wife. He wanted to believe in it.

'I can see why you have created this beautiful world,' said Long when his mind returned from the hell he was imagining.

'Would you help me to get there?' begged Gavin when his mind returned from the Fairyland.

Some moments ago that Long had realized his fate was decided by another man. Now this man was begging for his help. *I can make my decision.* 'Just get me some water.' Long was not sure if it would work but if it could, he saw no reason of deciding not to help.

Long walked over to the only wall in the room not covered by bookshelves. He took out the magic feather, dipped it in the cup of water Gavin have brought and began drawing. In less than a minute, he had drawn a doorway with an outlook of that endless flower field.

Gavin was amazed by Long's talent and skill. He couldn't believe that the talent he had created for Long was so real, so fascinating. Gavin was so struck that he just stood there motionless with open eyes and an open mouth.

'Now walk through it.' Long was urging Gavin as he knew that the doorway would vanish as the water dried up.

'It's a wall.' Long hesitated.

'You have to believe in it. Just close your eyes and step forward.'

Gavin took a deep breath and did as Long said. In fact, the instruction he was following, was the one he had written for Long just half an hour before; the instruction that had brought Long here. Gavin reached out his hands and stepped forward. He didn't crash into the wall. Instead he could feel a soft breeze blowing on his finger tips. He could feel the warmth of the sun on his face. He could smell the flowers. There was a soft carpet of grass underneath his feet. He just had to get across it. But before he could take a first step he heard a voice behind him, already as if from another world.

'Take the feather or you won't be able to come back.' Long pushed the feather into Gavin's back pocket.

Soon the field, the door and Gavin had vanished. Long was now alone in a world that wasn't his and Gavin was in a new world too. Would they regret not having thought hard enough on what it was they had chosen to do?

8

What if the man never comes back?

Gavin stepped across with his eyes closed. He knew he needn't open his eyes at once for even without looking, he was sure he was there. He could feel the wind and the sun; he could hear the vibrations of the insect wings; he could smell the daffodils and the lavender. He was still praying. But when finally he opened his eyes, it was not as he'd hoped: Sofia wasn't standing before him. He was in a dream-like place with grass up to his waist, and over here and there were forget-me-nots, buttercups, daffodils, bluebells, and every flower that you could name; all except for roses. Apart from the flying insects all around him, Gavin found himself alone. But Gavin knew, as we all know, that there were the tiny flower fairies who would be seen only if they wished to be seen.

Gavin began to hum one of the fairy tunes. He could tell from the sparkles among the flowers that hundreds of curious eyes were staring at him now. He moved on from one tune to another, from humming to singing and soon names were added to that hide and seek song. Those fairies hearing their names began to rise from their crouching positions as if they were being discovered in the game.

Gavin had not expected he could recognize them but they looked exactly as they were in his imagination. He waved to each one of them with a single finger and counted. 'Hanako, Marigold, Jasmine, Crisento, Cloris, Snowdrops, Acacia, Nalin, Zinnia, Alyssa, ... but where is Periwinkle?'

'Hey, are we supposed to know you, too?' asked Nalin. He was one of the two fairy boys Gavin had created.

'No, we have never met before.'

'Then how come you know our names?' Marigold, the one with a bright yellow skirt, asked after she had flown over and landed on Gavin's finger tip.

'And our songs?' added some other fairies as they came closer and hovered around him.

'I only know those two songs and you are the only ones I know.'

By this time, more fairies were flying over. Gavin couldn't recognize any of them. These newcomers had not been created by Gavin but there was no difference in general outlook between them and Gavin's own creations. Except in the eyes of Gavin, it was just one fairy community. Every fairy here knew each other and all of them shared the same songs, including the two created by Gavin. Who could say whether these fairies were older or younger than those Gavin had thought up? In role, demeanour, action—each was as individual and as much a fairy as any of Gavin's creation.

But Gavin didn't have time right now to think how fairies made or self-made might differ. He was just wondering where Periwinkle was. He was about to ask for her, when he was distracted by a flow of purple descending down along a spiral ray from above.

'Hey, you are looking for me?' The fairy in the purple skirt hovered daintily as she came to land on an orange poppy.

"Gavin was delighted to see Periwinkle."

Gavin was delighted to see the familiar short curly hair, big glassy eyes and a chubby face with the left dimple slightly deeper than the one on the right. Yes, she was Periwinkle, that kind-hearted fairy whom Gavin had created in his story with some features of his daughter when she was three.

'Pide vo neev zou!' Gavin greeted Periwinkle.

Periwinkle was surprised to hear Gavin speaking Mariwinklish. The fairies knew every earthy language but this was not actually a dialect of any culture. It was the secret code shared only between Princess Mariana and Periwinkle.

'Pide vo neev zou voo,' said Periwinkle, 'cuv xjo are zou apf xjere are zou gson?'

Gavin could remember the greeting lines but he did need some time to decode the other words by remembering, in each case, what the previous consonant in the alphabet had to be while the vowels remain unchanged.

'Ny . . . pane . . . it . . . Hawip. I an gson . . . junap . . . xormf.' Gavin had to speak a word at a time as he took some time to encode the words in his mind. Having shown that he knew her secret code, he decided to switch back to his own language, 'I am Gavin, from the human world.'

'From Mariana's world?'

'Not . . . really.' Gavin hesitated.

'You know Mariana?'

'Yes, of course. I know her as well as I know you.' Gavin was sure this time.

Periwinkle looked puzzled, 'but I don't know you?'

'Mariana was a brave princess and her lover, Egbert was the descendant of a heartless dragon. She went to look for the magical herb that could save Egbert, who was dying from a shrinking heart. Mariana found the herb in the garden of the Green-fingered Witch. And to get the herb, she had to give up her memory to the witch. That was the bargain. Since her memory was gone, she couldn't find her way home. She wandered on and got lost in Fairyland until finally she met you. You two became good friends and made up that secret language for fun. You found the secret way to get her out of Fairyland. You even tore your skirt among the rose bushes in the secret passageway.' Gavin was reciting his story fluently as if he was doing another presentation at the magazine meeting.

Periwinkle was surprised to hear every detail. She couldn't help laying her hand on the torn part of her skirt which Gavin had mentioned. It had already been mended and there were no observable stitches. It was a long time ago.

'How do you know all these things?'

'Because it's my story.'

'Your story?'

'Because I made up the story.'

'Of what actually happened to us?' Periwinkle's eyes brightened as she sought to clarify her understanding.

Gavin had intended to tell the fairies his identity so that they might feel grateful and affectionate towards him and so that they would help him. But now he began to hesitate. He remembered the disappointment on Long's face when he'd learnt that he was just a character in a story. Should he tell these merry fairies that they were only his creations? Did he have to tell them such a truth? His mind was changing.

'I mean I'm a writer in my world and I've written a story about fairies. It was such a coincidence that I also created a character called . . . .'

Before he could finish inventing this new story, Periwinkle had already interrupted excitedly, 'That's what I always sensed. I keep telling the others that I can sense some forces guiding our actions and thoughts. They just don't believe it. I thought we were in someone's dream but now I know, we are not dreamt of but written of.'

Now it was Gavin's turn to be surprised to see how his character reacted now that he was actually in conversation with her.

'Hey, come over to meet this man who dreamt, . . no, I meant . . . who wrote us.' Periwinkle turned around to call the others.

The other fairies came closer to examine Gavin.

'No wonder we don't know you but you know about us.' That was the other boy fairy, Crisento.

'Have a drink of our nectar.' It was Cloris who offered him the drink on a hibiscus leaf. Three other fairies were helping, each holding a corner.

Gavin took a sip. It was sweet but there was so little of it and Gavin found himself asking for more. He tried a variety of flower juices and soon he felt so relaxed in the peaceful environment, he found himself dozing off.

Where Gavin had left him, Long was now alone in the study. He couldn't believe that he would just let this man go through the doorway by himself. He should have followed him and looked after his magic feather. *What if the man never comes back? What if he is just happy to stay with his wife in that beautiful Fairyland forever? Then how am I going to get back to my own place and time? Or am I going to be trapped here forever?* Long began to worry and felt regret for having acted so impulsively but at that moment, he'd really been so touched that he'd had to help at once.

It only took a minute for his fear to dissolve, because as Long leant back despairingly on the big chair behind the desk, something on the desk caught his sight. It was the picture of a little girl behind a drum-like object; it was an object with colourful candles on top. Long took up that metal frame and touched the picture gently. The girl was smiling so heartily. Then as Long looked around, he noticed that there were many such framed pictures on the cupboards and shelves behind him. Pictures in this world were so real that it seemed people were trapped within the frames, as if they were trapped at some memorable instant. Most of the pictures in the room were of the same little girl though at different ages he could tell. That author man was in one or two of the pictures as well. There was also a nice looking young woman bearing the same sweet smile as the girl. She was in many of the pictures. Long could guess that she was the man's wife. Then the girl must be their daughter. Yes, he remembered now that the man had mentioned about his beloved daughter. Long felt more relaxed now for he was sure that he would return. Who would leave such a lovely girl behind?

There was nothing Long could do about going home but to wait for the man to return with his magic feather. While waiting, however, he could make some exploration in this world. Long knew this was a different world from his own. But how different was it?

The first things that caught his sight were the books on the desk and on the shelves. Long's father was a poor scholar so books were once his father's treasure but they were all sold after his death. Long did learn to read in his early years but it was his super memory and observant talent that accounted for the enhancement in the aftermath. Now with all these books in front of him, Long could not resist the urge to read all of them from cover to cover.

There were lots of books which Long picked up but put down at once since he had absolutely no idea what those strings of symbols meant. However, he did find something that interested him, some reference books on the desk which Gavin used lately to research on Chinese paintings and Chinese history. The former consisted of collections of Chinese paintings of different styles, at various times and from various artists. Long studied all these mini pictures with great appreciation though he found none of them comparable to the magnificent work of Master Sun. Finally, it was the Chinese history that attracted him most. He scanned through the history that he already knew and soon came to the part on the Ming Dynasty. He couldn't understand those years in numbers but he could recognize the name of his current ruler, the Yongle Emperor. Long found out that this emperor would move the capital from Nanjing to Beijing. This made him feel sad even though he had never liked the city too much. He kept reading and was excited to learn of this history in his future. But with every page he turned he felt more complicated emotions. This was especially so when he learnt that the Han people would lose control of the kingdom to a foreign tribe again. Long began to wonder what dynasty it was at present.

As Long turned the pages, he noticed the interesting symbols at the bottom and it didn't take him long to recognize the ten symbols and figure out how they combine to make up numbers. He realized the number 2010 on every page of Gavin's desk calendar and comparing those similar figures in the history book with it, he soon realized that Gavin's world was almost 600 years after his time.

Long examined everything around him closely, touching, shaking, smelling or listening. He was curious to know about everything especially after he realized that there was a six hundred year gap between the technology of his time and Gavin's. The first machine he was curious to learn about was the light emitting cupboard that he saw Gavin opening when he'd first entered the room. Long felt fascinated when he opened a white box full of cold air and full—yes full—of food and drinks. It must be to keep them fresh. How clever! He touched the cold metal objects in there but he didn't know what to do with them. But it was a hot day and like a small child he was tempted to go to that cupboard and open it every few minutes to cool himself down. He repeated the action until later he accidentally touched the power switch of the air conditioner remote on the desk. Immediately, he could feel a cool breeze blowing out from a rectangular box just below the ceiling of the opposite wall. He had no idea what that was but the cooler air made him feel more comfortable to explore.

Long started moving away from the desk area to other parts of the room. He was impressed by the bookshelves and the number of books filling them. He pulled out a book randomly and sat himself on the couch in front of the bookshelf. But it was so comfortable that he forgot his intention to read. He explored the couch in different ways, touching, bouncing, lying, sliding . . . . On it there were other small rectangular blocks with buttons. He pressed some of them tentatively, one at a time. Every time after he pressed a button, he turned around to see if any changes occurred in the room. He was expecting another discovery like that of the air conditioner. To his disappointment, most of them gave no observable effects. But there was one button, which moments after pressing, filled the room with voices and then a few seconds later crowds of people appeared at a great distance but within the frame of a big, black rectangle in front of him. Just as in those framed pictures on the desk, the people appeared so real. Were they actually trapped? They could move and they could talk but they couldn't come into the room. They didn't seem to know Long was there watching them. After the initial fright, since he felt no threat, he sat back again and attended to what these people were saying. Long pressed more buttons and discovered that one button could make their voices louder or softer. Another button could make different groups of people or animals or scenery appear in that black box.

In just an hour of television viewing Long had become a citizen of the twenty first century. There was much he could not understand, true, but there was also much he now knew about this new world he was in. Long had always liked to remember things and had always had a photographic memory. Things he was seeing now were so far beyond his imagination that at first he was not sure if this was a real world. It was later when he explored further around the house that he saw telltale resemblances between the details in the house and those in that framed world in the box. The impression he had from the latter helped guide him through some practical challenges in this new world. The first challenge came soon.

Gavin's mobile phone began to vibrate under his sleeve. Yes, it was that small black thing that Long had got hold of as a makeshift weapon when Gavin had come closer and closer. It was like an animal, but it couldn't really move; it could only wriggle. It was as if it were trying to speak but all it could manage was a low murmur. Long was so scared that he just opened the cool cupboard, put the phone in and closed the door. Then he could no longer hear the buzzing. When he opened the fridge later, the object lay inert and silent.

Not long after that, Long heard another ringing. It kept up and after a few times, there was a little girl's voice, 'Zoe is speaking but sorry, me and my dad are not home or we're too busy to pick up the phone, please leave your message.' By this time, Long was less scared. He traced the sound to the answering machine.

A light was flashing and soon came a woman's voice, 'Gavin, it's Edith. Where are you? I couldn't reach you but I hope everything's fine. If you're held up by something, it's okay. It doesn't matter you've missed today's meeting. We're almost done. Actually, I hope it's because you're on your way to Shanghai. By the way, I also called to let you know that we all like your "little authors' project". So go ahead. I'll wait for your details after the weekend. Call me when you're home.'

Long could remember that people framed in that black screen spoke to each other over the machine. He was thinking of how to reply but the woman was talking so fast that before he could tell her that Gavin was away, it was over. Long then remembered the mobile phone also. Now he recognized what it was. He opened the fridge but then he couldn't think what use he could make of it so he just left it there next to the cans.

Seeing those cans again, he couldn't resist the temptation to try one. He opened it in the way he saw in the TV commercial but instead of a big gulp, he just took a small sip first. It was so sweet and cool. He liked it. Of course, he was quite thirsty by now. So while Gavin was enjoying the flower juice in Fairyland, Long was enjoying the cold soda on his sofa. Long started to like this world.

9

How did you come here?

'Daddy. I'm back, . . .' Zoe called out once she was in the front door while Granny was still getting the keys out from her bag. Zoe was excited to be home. She missed her dad especially on Friday when she was picked up and taken home by Granny.

Every Friday, Gavin had to attend the regular meeting at the magazine office. Other than those few hours, he stayed home most of the time, writing his stories, busy with the house chores and taking care of Zoe. The meeting was usually just from two to five but he didn't like it because it overlapped with Zoe's pick up time. Even though she would attend the drawing class after school, that extra hour still wasn't enough to get him there in time.

'Daddy, . . .' Zoe shouted at the top of her voice, still taking off her shoes near the door. Zoe couldn't wait. Neither could Granny. Zoe had so many things from school to share with her dad. On the other four weekdays, she would have already gone through half of them while Gavin was driving her home or when they stopped by the supermarket.

'Daddy, are you home?' Zoe called again, as she was putting her shoes back in the shoe cabinet. There was still no response.

If Gavin was home, he would have been waiting in the living room or would have rushed out to give her a big hug already. Most probably he was a bit late today. It had happened a few times before but it wouldn't be more than half an hour. The traffic could be really bad sometimes after five.

Granny wasn't taking off her shoes and had no intention to do so. Sometimes she might stay for dinner or at least, she wouldn't miss the chance to talk to her son for a few minutes once a week. But she was in a hurry to leave today because she had to rush home to join Zoe's grandpa to get their things ready for the night flight to Australia. Gavin's sister was going to have a baby in a few days' time and the couple had planned to go and stay with her family for a month.

'Where's your daddy? I reminded him last night and he promised he would be home before six. He should let Kei Kei help.' Granny was already dialing Gavin's mobile number while she scolded him via Zoe. 'I don't suppose I should rely on his offer to drive me to the airport, either.' Granny kept grumbling while she was waiting for the phone to be connected.

'It's okay, granny. You better go. Daddy may be just a few minutes late.'

Granny could hear the connecting tone of Gavin's cell phone but no one was answering. 'What could keep him from just picking up the phone?' Granny was losing her patience.

'Maybe he's driving.' Zoe was trying to find excuses for her dad, hoping that granny wouldn't get angry with him.

'Hey, . . . voice mail again.' Granny was about to get angry but when she saw Zoe's innocent face and her apologetic gesture, she softened her voice to leave the message. 'Gavin, it's mum. I hope you're on your way back. Zoe's home. I have to leave now. Call you again. Bye.' Granny tried to hold her temper for she knew well that for Zoe, her dad was perfect. So she didn't want to upset her.

'I think I'd better go in case I need to spare some time to get a taxi.' Granny was sure that Gavin wouldn't let Zoe wait for long.

'Don't worry! I'm home already and daddy is on his way.'

'Okay! Zoe, I'm so sorry that I have to leave you alone.' But granny did hesitate for a moment, wondering if it was safe to do so.

'It's alright, granny. I promise I'll sit still to wait for daddy. Relax! We'll call you when daddy's home. Have a safe trip and remember to take lots of baby cousin's pictures for us. Bye!'

'I'll call you later!' Granny said on her way out.

Once Granny had left, Zoe rushed into her dad's study. She had decided to wait for him there to give him a surprise.

But it was Zoe who got the surprise. There was a man in the room.

Long was not as scary now as when Gavin first saw him. Knowing that he would meet a child, he had taken care of his appearance. He had combed his long, matted hair and tied it up in a pony tail. He'd also shaved for the first time after all these days of living in the wild. He was wearing Gavin's clothes so to make himself look more like the people he saw on TV and in Gavin's magazines.

Still Zoe almost screamed as she was not expecting a stranger in the room. Long greeted her at once, 'You must be Zoe. Nice to meet you.'

Long was holding his hands together like everyone does for 'Kung Hei Fat Choy' during the Chinese New Year. Zoe found it so funny that she forgot to scream. He knew her name and he was in her daddy's study room so he must be her daddy's friend.

'Are you my daddy's friend? Where is he now?'

'Yes, my little lady, I guess your daddy would consider me his friend. He knew me well since I was small.' Long was measured in his reply.

'Where is my daddy?' Actually Zoe was not interested to know the answer for the first question. She had assumed Long to be her daddy's friend that she was talking to him. She just wanted to know when her dad would be back.

'Yes, my lady. I have seen him a few hours ago. He asked me to stay and wait for him.'

'He's gone for the meeting, right? Friday, you know, it's his meeting day but he should be back very soon. Don't worry!' Zoe was actually reassuring herself. She remembered the phone call last night. She'd overheard him talking about a conference in Shanghai. But no, he wouldn't have gone for that or else he would have told her and made some arrangement.

'I am afraid not, . . .'

'Not what?'

'. . . . not . . . very . . . soon . . .' Long said slowly word by word, to buy himself some time in thinking how to explain the case to Zoe.

Zoe was just beginning to feel something wrong when she noticed that the red light on the answering machine was on. So she rushed to it and pressed the play button to see if her dad had left her any recorded message.

It was the voice of her daddy's editor. 'Gavin, it's Edith. Where are you? I couldn't reach you but I hope everything's fine . . . . I hope it's because you're on your way to Shanghai . . . . .'

Before Long could think of something to say, Zoe had offered her speculation. 'He's really away for the conference? I heard him saying that he wouldn't go.'

'Perhaps he had a very important reason.' Long tried to comfort Zoe as he saw her on the verge of tears.

'But he didn't even say goodbye.'

'Perhaps things just happened all of a sudden, too sudden to make better arrangements.'

'But at least he has arranged a friend to help here.' Zoe was prepared to forgive her daddy.

'Yes, if I was not here, he couldn't have gone.' Long was proud of having helped. He was wondering if Gavin had found his wife in the Fairyland by now.

Back in Fairyland, the fairies had been showing Gavin around, so he was seeing things that he had described in his story. But there were also other details beyond his descriptions. He spent happy hours with all the fairies, both the ones he had created in his story and the others that he couldn't name. They shared afternoon tea of nectar pancakes and berry shakes under the warm spiraling sunrays that gave no hint of direction. The fairies taught him songs that he didn't know and they sang to the rhythm of the cicadas. Then with the rise of the first of the evening stars, the fireflies joined in the party. Gavin was now dancing happily with his friends among these tiny flying lanterns.

Night crept in further and finally, they were too tired to sing or dance anymore. They sat down by a bonfire to share a dinner of honey cookies and roasted sunflower seeds served on the flower itself.

'How did you come here?' The curious fairy called Alyssa was the first one to ask him this question.

Like the loathsome but meant-for-good alarm clock, this question wakened Gavin from his sweet dream. He sprung up and looked around. He began to turn pale against the dark background. It was all dark but for the twinkles here and there from the stars, the fireflies and the sparkling eyes. The stars were orbiting along the domed surface he'd thought up and their positions kept changing and quickly just as he'd imagined. There were stars shooting across the sky in all directions and the fireflies and sparkles in the nearer distance seemed to move in just the same way. He felt as if he were trapped inside one of those snow globes people usually received as a Christmas present. Only there was no snow, just the stars that Gavin had put there.

He remembered the lines he had written in his story. 'No one can find the way out of Fairyland because there are no directions there. Actually no one attempts to find the way out. It's such a happy place, there's no need to keep track of time.'

But Gavin remembered that Zoe should be waiting for him at home. He had to leave at once, but how? For the first time since the afternoon, his initial excitement and joy began to give way to sensible fears. It was only now that he knew he couldn't remember how to get back to his world. He couldn't remember because those were his rules, those were the rules of Fairyland.

Gavin was still standing there in silence, wracked with doubt when the friendly Snowdrop asked another question. 'Why did you come here?'

It was then that he remembered what he was supposed to have come for. How could he have forgotten something so fundamental? 'My wife had got lost in Fairyland. I had to find her and bring her home.' Gavin was saying the lines that had been repeated numerous times in his mind. 'Had to find her. Had to.' It was as if these were instructions from the past. Over these years, they were repeated to offer some kind of consolation.

'Has anyone seen my wife? Her name is Sofia. She had a pointy face, dark brown eyes and curly hair to her shoulder . . . No, the time you met her, she wouldn't have had hair. She was wearing a rainbow coloured scarf on her head and a purple gown, you know, the kind of gown that people wear in hospitals.'

The fairies looked at each other, and one by one, they were all shaking their heads. They'd never heard of hospitals.

'But we could take you to see the queen. She might be able to help.' A fairy with red hair made the suggestion.

'You have a queen?'

'Yes, did you write about our Queen?' asked Periwinkle.

'No, I didn't know you had a queen'

'And you don't know all of us.' The fairy with a pointed nose pointed it out.

'Yes, so I didn't create Fairyland? So it does exist on its own?' Gavin recalled all the details he saw in this world that hadn't been in his descriptions. He remembered now that the whole creation had started from a postcard picture.

10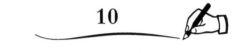

Never forget me, please!

Zoe and Long had settled down at the kitchen table. Zoe was serving him some Oreo cookies and milk. Long imitated the way Zoe ate her cookies. First, he licked all the cream from between the top and the bottom of the cookie. Then he dipped them in the milk before he ate them. He could see that was the proper way to eat such a snack. Zoe found it very amusing to see an adult eating in such a childish way. This cute act made her like Long. She giggled heartily and Long, for his part, liked her genuine laughter.

'Thank you for coming to help. And by the way, I'm sorry I forgot to ask your name.' After that giggling, Zoe remembered that she should act politely.

'My last name is Kwok and my name is . . . er . . . er . . . .' Long pretended to cough so as to buy himself some time. He had no intention to reveal his identity. Within that flash of a second, he could only think of people he knew so he borrowed the name from another house servant. 'My name is Ah Kei.'

'Kwok . . . Ah Kei . . . Oh, that's why people called you KK. Should I call you KK or Uncle Kwok?'

'Errrh . . . KK . . . Yes, KK will be fine.' KK—what a strange name, he thought, but Long could only react according to Zoe's lead. Before he could think of what he should do or say next, Zoe continued the conversation.

'I thought it was Auntie Kei Kei when Granny mentioned you offering to come and help. So you know my granny also? Are you my daddy's colleague? Or his old classmate? I've never heard my daddy mention you before. But actually my daddy has very few friends, I guess. Sometimes I ask him to go out and have fun with his friends but he always says that he prefers to stay with me. His job is quite lonely. You know, a writer spends most of his time writing by himself. I wonder if you . . .'

'I beg your pardon. Would you slow down a bit? I cannot follow.' Long was quite embarrassed to be not able to understand a little girl.

'I'm sorry. I keep making bah . . . bah . . . bah. My daddy always says I'm a chatter box and my teacher says so too. But I know they both enjoy talking with me.'

'Me, too.' And Long really meant it.

'And you know . . . .' Zoe was going to begin another round of non-stop talking.

Long had to stop her because there was something he really wanted to know. 'Sorry to interrupt but is this our dinner?' The cookies were nice but his stomach was grumbling. He had not eaten anything for hours.

'No, of course not. It's spaghetti night . . . but daddy's not here. Do you know how to make spaghetti?'

'S . . . pa . . . . get . . . ti . . . . Sorry I think I have not heard of it.' Long was trying to recall the TV he had watched.

'Not heard of it?' Zoe was puzzled that anyone didn't know about spaghetti. Now for the first time Zoe noticed that Long looked odd in his clothes. Her dad's shirt, all buttoned up to the top and her dad's shoes but without socks. The shaving was not complete. She was proud of her observation and analysis. She drew a conclusion. 'Oh, I know. I should have noticed that. You come from the mainland?'

'I am from Nanjing.'

'But where's your luggage?'

'Errrh . . . I was in a hurry . . . so you know . . .'

'Oh, I know! So you left your luggage in the taxi. That time, we were almost late for our plane and we also left one suitcase in a taxi. And we didn't have time to go back and look for it.'

'Yes, exactly!' Long began to realize that telling a lie wasn't so difficult.

'By the way, where's Nanjing?' Zoe knew very little about China. She had only heard of Beijing and Shanghai.

'It used to be the capital, a very prosperous place. It is located on the south bank of the lower reaches of the Yangtze River. It has . . .' Long was glad there's something he didn't need to lie about. But his voice soon died down since he had no idea of what changes the city had undergone over all these years. 'I'm not too sure now,' he muttered.

'Why?'

'Erhhh . . . I've been away for some time.'

'Oh. I see. But anyway, I've never been to China. There's one place I'd like to go.' Zoe took down a photo which was pasted on the fridge and showed it to Long. 'Here, Jiuzhaigou. My daddy and mummy went there for their honeymoon. Isn't it beautiful? I'll show you the album later. There are colourful lakes, limestone pools, . . . what else . . . ?'

'. . . . bamboo jungles, waterfalls, snow capped mountains, pandas, golden monkeys, tigers and many rare animals . . .'

Long continued as Zoe paused. He could recognize the place at once and he missed his animal friends.

'So you've been there?'

'In fact, I was living in the bamboo jungle with my friends for many years. Maybe if you and your daddy would like to come for a visit, I can introduce you to my friends.'

'Wow! You live in such a beautiful place . . . .'

That's how their friendship began. Long and Zoe had a very nice evening of sharing. Zoe instructed Long how to make the spaghetti and she helped just in the way she helped her dad. She found it quite unsurprising that Long should know nothing of the modern kitchen and its gadgets; after all he'd come from a remote and primitive place, in nature reserve area where he lived with the animals. The spaghetti was a bit overcooked but they liked the dinner just the same. They really enjoyed each other's companionship.

Zoe told Long about her friends at school and Long told her about his fun with the animals. 'Ah! I know my daddy must have got the inspiration from you when he wrote the story of Long. He had some animal friends in the bamboo jungle, too.'

After dinner, Zoe showed Long the pictures she'd drawn. Long liked them at once. Each stroke showed confidence and the use of colours was bold. She didn't really follow any rules in the overall framing, relative scales or perspective but Long liked the work for its freshness. The pictures were so lively, and he particularly liked those big smiles on the faces of the people, of the animals, of the flowers and the sun. Each picture seemed to be telling a story and it was so imaginative. Then there was the picture of the family. There was a man with a checked shirt and a nice looking woman with curly hair to her shoulders. Each was holding one hand of the little girl between them. Each of them was wearing a crown on the head and wearing a big smile. Long loved the pictures. He loved this talented young artist and her style.

Long also drew for Zoe, not with water on the table. For the first time, he used her water colours and drew on paper, a picture of Jiuzhaigou from his memory. The colours impressed Zoe very much. She thought Long was one of the greatest artists in the world. She was probably right. And why wouldn't she be? This was not just a comment from an ordinary child. In books Zoe has seen pictures from a lot of great artists.

It was almost bed time. For Zoe, it was her valuable story time. This reminded her of her daddy so she phoned him. Long began to worry also. He had not expected Gavin to be away for so long. He began to wonder if Gavin would be able to find his wife.

Of course, no one picked up the phone. And because it was still in the fridge nobody could hear it vibrating inside. It was only now Zoe began to worry. It never happened before that her daddy just disappeared like this without even a phone call. She turned to Long, 'Why didn't he answer the phone?'

Long said nothing. Then Zoe tried to draw Long's attention with the question again. 'What kept him from the phone?'

'Someone truly important to him'

Gavin was really talking to a VIP. He'd been brought to the Queen of the fairies.

'You are from the 'other' human world.' said the Queen.

'I am from the human world. But . . . wait . . . what do you mean by 'the other'?' Gavin was puzzled.

'We are not supposed to go to the human world but some of us did find the secret passageway through the rose bushes.' While saying so, the Queen, took a glance at Periwinkle before she continued. 'We can get to that human world if we want to.'

'That's where Mariana and Egbert live.' Periwinkle whispered in Gavin's ears.

'Besides that, occasionally, we also have visitors from another human world. That's a human world far separated from us in space and time. Only in dreams, some people from that world may accidentally drift over here. But none of them ever came as far as you've come.'

'I think I had dreamt about this place before.' Gavin could remember now.

'That's no surprise. We do meet dreaming minds every now and then. But they won't stay for long. Those of us on guard will guide them back to their bodies.' The Queen was quite sure about that.

'What if they don't have a body to return to?'

'Then they will drift on.' The Queen was still sure as she looked into the distance.

'Has anybody ever stayed?' Gavin asked with hope.

'Nobody stays because no "body" can come . . . .' This time the Queen wasn't sure. She flew around Gavin and gave him a closer look before she continued. 'Except you. I don't know how you manage to come so far but for sure you are not dreaming now. You are here both body and spirit.'

'I came here through a magic doorway. It was a door drawn with a magic feather. I came here to look for my wife.'

'Does she have a body to return to?'

Gavin was silent. He knew the answer.

The Queen knew the answer as well. 'You won't be able to find her. First of all, we don't know if she is here or not. Even if she did come, this is such an endless place that we won't be able to locate her. If she's really here, she will by now have forgotten who she is. But I can assure you, she must be happy if she is here. You should know that.'

'But not anymore. I would like to leave. I have to go home. She has to come home too.'

'You have to go home because you have a body but what's the use of bringing her spirit home even you could find her. Sometimes it is better to forget.'

Gavin was silent again. He knew that it was true. He couldn't forget and that hurt every time when he remembered the things they had done or not done. If Sofia had forgotten about him then she should be at peace.

Zoe and Long were looking through the albums now. Zoe insisted that she wouldn't go to sleep. She would stay awake to wait for Gavin's call. When finally the phone rang, she rushed to pick it up, 'Yes, the princess is speaking.'

Immediately her smile disappeared as she found out that it was granny on the other end. 'Zoe, my little princess. You sound so happy. You are having a good time with your daddy? No wonder you two forgot to call me. Now put your dad on the phone.'

'Errr . . . He's in the shower.' Zoe lied because she didn't want to make granny worried.

Long was staring at her, shaking his head unbelievably at her quick wit to lie. But she was quite proud of that. When she spotted a little red spot on Long's hair, she even made the lie better. 'He's got spaghetti sauce all over his hair.'

'Okay, then I'm not going to wait for him. I've to get on the plane and switch off the phone now. Tell your dad that I've called and I'll call again on arrival.'

'Okay. I will tell him. Take care. Have a safe trip.'

After the phone call, she led Long to the bathroom and handed him a towel and a pair of her dad's pyjamas. 'Take a bath now.'

'I don't need a bath.'

'You need. There's spaghetti sauce on your hair. I'm not lying this time.'

Before she left the bathroom, she turned to Long again for assurance. 'And you will stay until daddy comes home, right?'

'Yes, for sure.' Long assured her and actually where else could he go without his magic feather.

By the time he came out from the bathroom, Zoe had already fallen asleep on the sofa among some books. She'd been preparing to ask Long to read to her. Long picked up the books that had fallen on the floor. A bookmark fell out from one of the books. It was from the one in which Gavin had shown him the illustration of Fairyland.

It was a printed postcard of a water colour picture. It was a view from behind of a young girl standing amid a wide field of pastel purple. Here and there were dots of other colours over the field. The girl was wearing a purple dress, the colour of which merged into the field. Her head was tilting up to the sun's rays from above. Her hands were stretching out, each holding a corner of a big rainbow scarf behind her. The scarf was flying in the wind and so were some flower seeds and petals.

"It was a postcard of a young girl in a field of wild flowers."

Long turned the card over and saw handwriting that was neat, except with one word that had obviously been added to the front of the last line by another person.

> 'Last night in my dream
> I got lost here
> I know you will look for me
> That's what I fear
> Before I forget
> I whisper to the breeze
> Tell him my loving dear
> **<u>Never</u>** Forget me please'
>
> Forever yours,
> Sofia.

Now Long knew why Gavin had insisted to look for Sofia in Fairyland.

11

That's why I've been stuck here

Gavin bade farewell to the Queen and all the fairies. He knew he would miss the place but he also knew it was time to go and let go. Only that, things didn't happen as smoothly as he had expected.

When Gavin tried to pull the magic feather out from the back pocket of his jeans, he found out that it wasn't there. He remembered that Long had pushed it in his pocket at the last moment. He was sure he could feel it before but not anymore. Gavin didn't know when and where that feeling of the feather in his pocket had just gone. He'd been so overwhelmed with the magic that he'd not checked once since he'd stepped through the door. He was stupid to have not taken care of such a precious thing. He must have dropped it but when and where?

'Is there any other way I can return to my world?' Gavin was hoping that the fairies and the Queen would be able to help.

'As I've told you, we don't know how to get to your world physically. We can guide your mind back if it's just drifted over here in a dream but we've never seen a physical body from your world before. I'd like to help very much but I'm sorry I don't know how. You can only return through the way you came here.' The Queen's answer threw him into real panic.

'A feather . . . . , my feather . . . . did anyone see my magic feather? . . . . It's red and green and blue and . . . no . . . the colours keep changing . . . like a rainbow.' Gavin was running madly from one fairy to another.

The fairies were keen to help but they couldn't understand this agitated man. A fairy sprinkled some blue dust over Gavin to soothe him. Finally, he calmed down and told them the whole story.

Several 'days' had passed but Gavin was still stuck helplessly in the Fairyland. He and the fairies searched in the flower field inch by inch but it was in vain. Gavin began to suspect that Long might not have really put the feather in his pocket. *He might have got it back at the last moment so that he could be free of my control. By now, he would have returned back to his world or gone anywhere he wanted.*

Gavin could understand Long's disappointment and anger in realizing that he was just a character and had no control of his own life. Gavin had similar feelings in those days when he'd felt so helpless in relation to his own fate. So it was natural that Long would seize the opportunity to fight for his own autonomy instead of sitting back to await his creator's decision to grant him a good ending. In fact Gavin had really thought of an ending that would disappoint Long. It was one in which Long would lose everything since he would become greedier and greedier since getting the magical power. Gavin believed that it was human nature that the more one had, the more one desired. But that had just been a first thought. Gavin had discarded the idea for he would not write something to disappoint Zoe or other fairy tale lovers.

This was despite the fact that by now Gavin was quite confident in his beliefs regarding human greed. He had acted exactly the way Long had under the same spell. Gavin had been overwhelmed to realize that he had that power to work a miracle. That's why he had come here, thinking that he could bring a dead person back to life. If Long deserved to lose everything for the abuse of such magical power in the original plot, then Gavin deserved to face the same loss in reality. Gavin began to fear what negative consequences were lying ahead of him.

Gavin's fear grew as he watched the sky shifting from dusk to dawn and dawn to dusk. He was not thinking of Sofia anymore but every second, he was concerned only about what had happened or would happen to Zoe. He couldn't let her lose both parents. He was really anxious to go but now one whole week had passed and he was still stuck here.

Luckily, time in Fairyland was not running as it was back in Gavin's home. Sometimes a minute there was a minute here, true, but sometimes days would pass for Gavin in Fairyland, while only a few seconds ticked by for Long and Zoe. So while it was a torturing week for Gavin, back in the real world, Long and Zoe were still spending their first night together. Zoe had been long in bed by the time Long fell asleep reading Gavin's story about Fairyland.

Long was not sure if the book had grown in size or he had been shrunk. The only thing he saw was that illustration of Fairyland right in front of him. There was nothing else, just a big picture of that endless field of colours. For over a minute, the endless sky and flower sea took his breath away. He stood there speechless and motionless. Finally, he took a deep breath and the sweet scent of the flowers was inviting him to come forward. He moved towards the flower field and the next thing he felt was the gentle touch of the grass on his arms and the kiss of the breeze on his face. Long was now walking amidst a sea of flowers and long grass. He began to hear bells and songs and after a blink, he could see fairies every here and there. But they all seemed too busy to care about him.

The fairies were flying from flower to flower as if busy bees collecting nectar. But actually they were looking for something else. They flew close and over every flower just to look inside. They didn't land on any but keep moving on. Long found it very interesting to walk around and observe these tiny winged creatures. Then when he almost tripped and looked down as a reflex to see where he was going, he was surprised to find even more fairies flying amidst the long grass at very low altitude, around his legs. They must be looking for something on the ground, he thought. He crouched down to observe them closely.

After a while, Long saw a pair of legs approaching. He got up and found himself face to face with Gavin who was surrounded by a group of busy fairies. Each man was surprised to see the other again at this moment in this place, but each had different feelings.

Long was happy to meet Gavin. It was like seeing a friend a long way from home. The further from home you are the less close that friend needs to be for you to find joy in sharing. Long was especially glad to see Gavin since he might be the only person who could share his excitement here. Who else would know this fairy place?

Gavin's feelings were more complicated. As the days passed and he couldn't find the feather, he had become more and more certain that Long had taken it back at the last moment. And now Long's appearance verified his speculation. If it wasn't by the magic of the feather, how could he have got here? Gavin's anger with Long had grown to the stage where he really didn't know what he should do with him in the plot of his story. So Gavin was furious with Long but at the same time glad to see him for at least he could confront him now. *No, forget about confrontation.* Gavin reminded himself to control his anger. *Having that magic feather in hand, Long had the upper hand. Without his help, I might never be able to return to my daughter.*

'It's amazingly beautiful here! No wonder you're not ready to return yet.'

Long's genuine expression sounded a mockery to Gavin. He would like to hit him right on the nose to wipe the smile off his face. But a second thought suppressed his fire of anger. *Why should Long be here when he could have been free already? He came here just to make fun of me? Or he might have felt regret for what he had done. So he has come to fetch me home.* Gavin wondered which the case was, and he was ready to believe in the latter explanation for he had created Long a kind-hearted person. He would rather forgive Long and forget the whole matter than ask for an explanation.

'Thank you for coming to get me. I'm ready to go now.'

'I didn't come for you. I didn't mean to come. I don't know why I'm here. But it's good that I have met you or

I might also get lost.' Long looked around the place. He would like to explore further but he knew that Gavin might be anxious to go. Long also feared that if he couldn't resist the temptation to stay a little bit longer, he might never be able to resist that temptation later. So, he took another deep breath of the sweet fresh air to bid the place goodbye. 'Okay let's go.'

Gavin patted Long on the shoulder as a gesture to indicate his forgiveness and gratitude. Long took it as a sign to show the sharing of their feeling for this secret place. For the first time, he felt Gavin to be a friend, he felt there was no boundary between worlds. Future and past, one story, another, inside and out—all were here.

But what a pity! The two men's good feelings lasted only for a moment.

The next minute both men were waiting for the other to take out the magic feather to draw the door to take them home. Each looked at the other, with the understanding or actually misunderstanding of that reluctant feeling to leave such a wonderful place.

'Okay, we really have to go. Zoe's been waiting for days.'

'For days? You're exaggerating. But anyway, yes, she is waiting. Let's go'

This time each could sense that the other was waiting for him.

Long recalled the scene of the fairies looking for something. A bad feeling rose and he couldn't wait to clarify his worry. 'Where's my feather?'

'I don't have your feather.'

'What do you mean? I lent it to you. I put it into your back pocket so that you could use it to come back.' Now, from the look on Gavin's face, Long knew that Gavin had lost his feather.

'But then you changed your mind and took it back at the last moment.' Finally Gavin poured out the suspicion that had been in his mind.

Long was angry to be accused for something he hadn't done. 'If I took it back, then how will you be able to get back?'

'That's why I've been stuck here and you can be free. Isn't this what you wanted?' Gavin couldn't control his anger now.

'I should have taken it back. Why should I have helped such a selfish, arrogant and ungrateful person? In fact, why should I have put my precious feather in your pocket in the first place? You didn't even remember to ask for it.' Long was really disappointed with this man whom he had considered a friend a moment ago.

'But if you didn't have the feather, then how did you get here?' Seeing the worry, anger and disappointment on Long's face, Gavin began to doubt his suspicion. But he still needed an explanation.

'I've told you already I don't know why I'm here or how. I just walked into this world. And I know you're not the only person stuck here now.'

But Long was wrong, Gavin could see. Long must only be dreaming. Gavin was still the only person who would stay. One on each side, two fairies were each ringing a bluebell in Long's ears. No sound was heard but the next moment, Gavin was shocked to see Long disappearing right in front of his eyes. One of the bluebell fairies explained, 'It was just his mind drifting in.' The other fairy added, 'We should have sent him back earlier when it was still a sweet dream.'

Gavin knew this would not work for him. Now Long was gone, he felt a loss. *Would Long be able to come again in another dream? Could I visit my home in a dream?*

Before Gavin could ask further, he heard the cheering voices of Periwinkle and some other fairies approaching. He could see even from a distance that the fairies were holding a rainbow coloured feather above their heads. Gavin was overjoyed to see the magic feather again.

'We found it under the hydrangea bushes. It must have been blown over there by the wind.'

So I was careless to have dropped the feather. And shame on me, I had falsely accused Long. He was right. I am too arrogant, selfish and ungrateful to deserve any help. I owe him a sincere apology. Gavin was pondering what he could do to pay back this friend. He could make things happen in Long's story according to Long's wishes. This arrogant author just hadn't realized that things might not always happen as one willed.

12

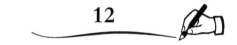

How could I be not real?

'I want to go home.' These were the last words in Long's heart and which still lingered in his mind when he woke up on the crouch in Gavin's study. Long opened his eyes and saw Zoe standing by his side, with a pan in one hand and a spatula in the other. *It was just a dream but why couldn't I just wake up on the tummy of Ding Ding or in the shade of the bamboo with Kit Kit on my chest. Am I still in a dream? When would I wake from it?*

'It's Saturday! Let's have bacon for breakfast!' Zoe was hitting the pan with the spatula when she saw Long, still caught up in his thoughts.

Zoe seemed very excited. Was Gavin back already? Did Gavin wake up with me from the same dream? Long got up and followed Zoe as she pulled him out to the living room and then into the open kitchen. He was looking around for Gavin. He was still so angry with this man that he wished he would never see him again. But immediately he regretted wishing things so.

'Since daddy's not here, can you fry me some bacon for breakfast?' Zoe was standing on a stool, getting the bacon out from the freezer.

So Gavin was not back yet. Was it really the case that that arrogant man had lost my feather and got stuck or was it just a dream? What if it was real? How am I going to tell Zoe what has happened, that her dad has got lost in Fairyland like her mum? And how am I going to return to my place?

'Did daddy call last night after I fell asleep?'

'Erh . . . yes.' *What am I going to tell her?* 'Errh . . . He said that he was in . . . . errh . . . in the wood. He was going to write errh . . . write stories about monsters and fairies in the wood . . . . Errh . . . . he said he might not be able to call again for some time.' So telling a lie was not that difficult. Once it started, it just developed on its own. And Zoe helped to fill up all the gaps.

'He's doing research in the wood? So isn't he at the conference?'

'No, . . . I mean . . . yes, he mentioned the words conference and research . . . .'

'Oh, so it was part of the program, a group research?'

'Yes, as a group. He's not alone. He's fine.'

'Why didn't he tell me beforehand?'

'He didn't expect it. You know, things may happen out of expectation.' Long was certain with this line.

'Yeah . . . and I think it's good for him. If he knew it before, he wouldn't have gone. I think he needs a break. Granny always says that she can take care of me for a few weeks and that he should go on a vacation. He has devoted all his time to me . . . . But you know, I can look after myself . . . . Did he say when he will be back?'

'A few days . . . it will take him just a few days'

A few days should be enough. I just need a few more days to confirm if it was a dream or it is true that he will never return. I need a few more days to think clearly how I am going to tell this little girl. Whatever it was Long would have to tell Zoe. He couldn't lie to hide the secret from her forever. And it was not only Gavin's problem if he'd really lost the feather. Long would not be able to return to his world either. He needed a few more days to prepare for the worst.

Perhaps the worst thing for Gavin was to realize that even with the feather, he couldn't return home. For a whole day, Gavin had been trying to draw the doorway. He was never good at drawing but it needed not be beautiful. Just an arch should be fine. Gavin thought. But it wasn't easy even to make a simple stroke. He could never dip enough water to finish the whole arch. By the time he was drawing a second stroke, the first one had almost dried up. It was never a complete picture. Gavin tried to make it smaller. The size shouldn't matter. He could just crawl over but it still dried up faster than he could manage to complete it. He kept bumping against the tree on which he was drawing.

The fairies helped by spraying water on the lines but this didn't work either. Gavin could see the full picture now but as it wasn't drawn by the feather, it remained a picture. He couldn't get through it. It had to work through the feather. He only managed to get his finger across when he drew a small circle, slightly bigger than a coin. By the time the sun set in Fairyland, the biggest circle he'd managed to produce and keep was the size of a cup and it had remained for just two seconds.

Gavin realized that it was impossible for him to do the job. It would be impossible for any real person to do it. Long could do it because he was a story character. Gavin had created him with such extraordinary talent and skill. Long was from a fairy tale!

But I'm real. I'm not just a character. Since after breakfast, Long had been reading his own story over and over. And the thought lingered.

After breakfast, Zoe had begged Long to read her the story, 'Long and the Magic Feather' from the beginning. Long scrolled down the pages on the computer as Zoe had instructed him. For the first time, he was reading a summary of his past.

'. . . . *With the idea in his mind, Long drew a doorway . . .*' Long paused. He knew exactly what was written next that he didn't even want to spot the words. He scrolled up the page, sighed and reluctantly announced, 'That's it. No more.'

'That's it? Oh! I thought daddy would have finished the whole story. But anyway I know what will happen. Long will return to draw the picture for the girl before it was too late and they will have a happy ending.' This was what Long had expected, too.

When Zoe was about to comfort Long who seemed to be upset by the story, the phone rang. Her grandparents were now calling from Australia to check if everything was alright.

While Zoe was making up stories to cover her daddy's irresponsible disappearance, Long was reading his story to himself again and again.

That's it, that's my life so far, all within those few pages. Long would have summed up his story in more or less the same way if he was going to tell anyone. But that wasn't all. Long knew it all well, because in his memory, he did live through every minute and every second. It wasn't only that he lived but he ate, he slept, he worked, he thought and he felt. He didn't only eat, but he chewed and he swallowed mouthful by mouthful, sometimes with sauce dripping on his clothes. It wasn't just that he slept but he snored and he dreamt, waking up sometimes with sweat over his body or tears on his face. Sometimes when he chopped wood a splinter stuck into his finger and often cinders blackened his nose. He met people not mentioned in the story. He said things not included in the dialogues. His thought and feeling were more sophisticated than described over the pages. Long really could not accept the fact that that he was created. That he was merely a character in a story. *I'm real. I'm not just a character. I've just been living in another world or at another time. And now I may have to live here forever after.*

'KK! . . . KK!' Long was too absorbed in his own thinking to hear Zoe calling him. Besides, he was still not so used to being called by this name.

Finally, Zoe had to wave right in front of his eyes to draw his attention. 'Hey, what're you thinking? Are you day dreaming? . . . So I can see that we have one more thing in common now.'

'I'm sorry I didn't hear you. I was just thinking about what I'm . . . no, what we're going to do afterwards.' By afterwards, Long was referring to the future days that he might have to stay.

'Afterwards? At half past nine, we are going to the creative writing workshop. Did daddy tell you about that? Hadn't he asked you to bring me there and did he ask you to substitute for him?' Long's puzzled expression gave the answers.

'No . . . oo? He shouldn't have forgotten about that. I'm really angry with him now. He just left without saying goodbye and he didn't even remember about his workshop.'

'His workshop?'

'Yes, daddy was planning to organize a "little author project". He worked with our teacher to help us in writing a story to be published in his magazine.

'Little author project? Oh! I remember now. Someone called E-dit . . . E-dith . . . has asked your dad to go ahead with it.' Long had absolutely no idea what was going on. He'd just managed to recall what he had heard through the answering machine.

But Zoe was impressed that Long knew about it. She assumed that Long must be involved in the project as well since even her dad might not have got the news of the approval. 'So you are also working at the magazine? You must come to tell the good news to my friends and help us to develop our ideas.'

'But I don't know . . .'

' . . . the way to school? Don't worry. We can take the bus or the MTR. Hmm . . . It's better to take the bus because we can see more things.'

'But your daddy asked me not to leave the house.'

'What? Oh, I see. It must be your first time in Hong Kong and he's afraid that you'll get lost. But don't worry. I know the way to school. After that, we can go to the shopping mall near the school. We can do everything there, lunch at McDonalds, go to the cinema, eat pop-corn, go ice-skating, check if there are any new good books in the bookstore . . .' Zoe was used to the routine, only that today she had a new companion. And this time she could be the one to lead. She was excited about that. 'Now let me go and get ready for our day of adventures.'

The thought of leaving the house and actually going out to see this world cheered Long up. So far, he hadn't even gone near the window to see what was behind the curtains. Till now, Long hadn't had a strong incentive to see a world where he had no part to play. Frankly, he was also scared of a world he knew nothing of. But now he was determined to overcome that fear. He was going to explore and to experience life in this world. *How could I be not real if I am actually experiencing things in it?*

13

It will not be too bad even if I have to stay

'Remember to bring your Octopus card[4]!' Zoe was reminding Long authoritatively of what her daddy used to remind her when they were leaving the house.

'I beg your pardon.'

'Sorry, I'm just saying what my dad would say. So you don't have the card?'

But Zoe saw her daddy's card in the tray on top of the shoe cabinet. It was lying in its regular place, together with the coins and keys so he wouldn't forget to bring them when going out. But he had forgotten it this time? Under the tray, there were also two movie tickets. He really had planned to take her to the cinema. As usual he bought the tickets in advance to ensure she wouldn't get disappointed in case all the good seats were taken. He must have really left in a hurry. But Zoe was too excited about her day of adventures to think any more about it.

---

[4]   It is a widely used, rechargeable stored value smart card for making electronic payment in Hong Kong, on almost all public transports and many supermarkets, chain stores, retailed shops and fast food restaurants.

She took the card, some coins and the keys just as her daddy did. 'You can take my daddy's card. It's very useful, like a magic wand. And take some coins also. There are things that the magic card can't work on. And I'll keep the keys.' Zoe was proud to be the key keeper.

Long was a bit nervous but also very excited when he stepped out of the front door. The day before, Long had had the same feeling when he'd stepped through that magic doorway. So this was the second time he'd had the feeling. But now, through the door, to his surprise he saw only corridors. So this was still not 'outside' yet. He could see other doors but no terrace. He followed Zoe, turned round the corner and stopped in front of a different door. Zoe pressed a button on the wall and they waited for a while. Long was curious but he thought it would be better not to show too much of his ignorance so he tried to act naturally.

Long had no fear when he followed Zoe into the small room. And then, a moment later, he felt a strange sensation—as if he was moving although he wasn't going anywhere. And then, with Zoe, he was counting down those numbers from 27 to a symbol that looked like 6. He was just curious why they had to go into such a small room. When he was about to ask, the door opened. He stepped out and saw it was a different place from where they entered. So, had they been moving? Was this another magic doorway? When they went out of the building, Zoe pointed for him to the windows of their apartment on the 27th floor. Long felt a delayed nausea as he imagined that small room descending from such a height within the space of a minute. He looked around. There were all these tall buildings everywhere. It was as if he was surrounded by a gang of tall monsters.

Zoe was proud to be able to give the road safety instructions to Long. She wasn't quite sure why he needed to be told such things. But then she remembered he was from somewhere remote and primitive. It was not too difficult for Long to remember what to do. Walk when the light was green and stop when it was red. Once they left the estate area and really got on the street, Long could see what Zoe meant when she said Hong Kong was a busy city. There were lots of people and lots of fast moving monsters of different sizes. Long knew they were kinds of vehicles, only that they were much faster than the sedan chairs and the horse carriages. Long had no problem crossing the first street when the light was already green and all the cars had stopped. He marched across like those people in front of them. But while waiting at the next crossing, cars were dashing by in front and people were pressing close from behind. He couldn't suppress the fear that a little push might have him totally squashed by one of these wheeled monsters. Most awesome of all were those two-levels gigantic monsters stuffed with people? How could those people remain standing at ease packed inside such a fast moving box? Not long after Long raised the question, he had the chance to step onto one of such boxes to find his own answer.

The experience was not totally negative. It was just new and he just needed some time to adapt to it. Zoe took out her octopus card and pressed it against a box as they got on. Long followed her and did the same with his 'magic wand'. The coolness inside the monster soothed Long at once and when it became less crowded, he could start enjoying the view. He was just a bit dizzy. He told himself he could get used to it. By the time he got off, recalling the distance he had travelled and now feeling the heat and sweat walking on the street, he'd started to think that this monster called 'bus', was actually quite a friendly creature.

Within the five minutes' walk from the bus stop to her school, Zoe introduced to him three more friendly monsters. The first was a shy little monster hiding behind the wall with buttons on its body. Long was curious to see people getting colourful paper out from its mouth.

'It's called ATM. It's very rich. It'll give you the money if you press the right buttons. But I can't demonstrate now. We need another magic card.'

'Money?' Long touched the coins in his pocket. Of course it was money. Although in his own time, money meant coins, Long knew that in earlier dynasties there had been a kind of money made of paper. And here it was again.

Turning the corner, the two of them came upon a stout monster with bottles and cans inside.

'Are you thirsty? Let's get a soda from the vending machine.'

Another monster? Why did all things in this world seem to be rectangular with buttons and numbers on their fronts? But Long liked pressing the buttons. He had already got the idea that all the buttons in this world were meant to make life easier. Zoe asked Long to hold her up so she could press one on the top row. Then she put her magic card near the position of the monster's heart. A bottle tumbled out of its tummy. Long did the same. He chose the soda he had tried in Gavin's study. A cold soda was definitely something Long would miss after he returned to his world.

The third of the monsters was even bigger than the other two. In fact it was two monsters together—twins. They were not rectangular boxes but looked like stairs.

'Let's take the escalator.'

Zoe held his hand. They just needed to step on the monster's back. Soon they were carried all the way up to the footbridge. Then coming down the back of another of these twins, they found themselves close to Zoe's school.

Long was getting used to the environment, tall buildings and elevators, fast moving vehicles and people, hustle and bustle, glass and metal, dust and light, screens and posters, buttons and numbers. They could all be scary and it would have been very scary to be left alone here. But thanks to Zoe, everything became fun and interesting. Long could imagine viewing the world through her eyes to find everything positive.

Zoe was such a considerate and kind hearted child, so different from her selfish and arrogant dad. If one day, Long could forgive Gavin, it would surely be because he had no better way to pay back all the thanks he already owed the little girl. Zoe was holding his hand throughout the whole journey to make him feel secure. Thinking that he was from a faraway village, she could understand his unease but she spoke no words to remind him of the fear or make him feel embarrassed. She just kept talking to distract him from the suffocating feeling on the bus or the dizziness he felt on the street from the fact that there was simply too much to see. Zoe was like a little tour guide, telling Long all the interesting aspects of whatever it was he could see.

'You know what that big, round thing is? . . . . Mmm, yummy, yummy. That's called pizza. We must take you there at least once before you leave.' It was just one of the advertisements on their way. And of course, there were also hamburgers, fried chicken, ice-cream, sushi, ... *So this place seemed to be a paradise with all kinds of delicious food. At least they looked delicious from the pictures.* Long might not have a chance to try all but he felt contented just looking at Zoe's expression while she was describing them.

'Oh! That's Doraemon! Do you have this cartoon in . . . . I forgot the name . . . . anyway in your place? . . . . He is a robot cat from the future. He has a lot of magical stuff. The thing I like best is his magic doorway. It can let you go to anywhere you wish . . . .' *So that's where her dad got the inspiration from? Why didn't Gavin just borrow the door from this blue . . . . cat? A cat?*

' . . . . You can even travel in time. Can you imagine? It's so cool! . . .' Zoe paused when she realized that she was doing all the talking. But she could tell that Long enjoyed listening to her. Still, as her teacher always said, we should give the chance for others to speak also. So this time she asked and waited patiently for the answer. 'Is there any place, any time, you would like to go?'

To Nanjing, on the date I went into that big mansion for the first time. Long had a definite answer in mind but he didn't say anything. He hadn't expected that he was meant to respond. But realizing that Zoe was still waiting for a response, he made something up to please her. 'To the future when you get married.'

'Oh, no. Please don't say that. We don't want to know about our future. It will not be mysterious anymore. But you don't need to wait for a long time, maybe twenty years. I will invite you to my wedding'

Zoe also talked about her happy and funny moments here and there that she had with her dad or her friends. Her world was so complicated but her picture of it was so simple and life was wonderful for her. Long began to like the city. *Be optimistic! After all, it will not be too bad even if I have to stay.*

No, I couldn't stay for even one more day. But time flies. Three days had passed in Fairyland. Of course, Gavin had no idea that time was running much faster here than elsewhere. Gavin noticed that the colour of the feather was not changing so frequently. He might have worn it out. So he gave up trying to draw with the feather. Anyway he wouldn't be able to do it. His last hope was that Long might come again in another dream. He was the only one that could draw the doorway to save him. But what if the feather didn't have enough magic left to make more than one doorway?

Now as Gavin had nothing to do, not looking for Sofia, not looking for the feather, not trying to draw the doorway, time suddenly ran much slower. He had plenty of time to reflect on himself and have negative thoughts. *What was Long doing in his world? Would he harm Zoe?* He should have asked about her last time when Long appeared in his dream. Gavin felt regret for everything he had done—coming to Fairyland, leaving Long at his home, interrupting Long's life and hopes, suspecting his friend's integrity, not asking about Zoe. It seemed that he hadn't done one right thing or made one right decision. The more he thought the more doubts he had about himself.

Perhaps people did get lost in Fairyland. Some lost their way, others lost track of time. Gavin lost his confidence.

14

Let's write an adventurous story

At the writing workshop, Long was impressed by the confidence and creativity of these young students when they shared their written stories. There were elements Long was not familiar with but he just let his imagination be led along by these young creators and their pictures.

'One day when the wolf woke up, he saw a sword. He picked it up and . . .' A wolf as the main character, was something Long would not have imagined.

' . . . the tree can do a lot of tricks. The tree can move too. One day I went in the forest . . .' An eight year old girl told a story of playing hide and seek with a special tree.

' . . . I walked through the mirror and I got to the fairy world of Cinderella and I turned into a boy . . . .' Of course, Long had no idea who Cinderella was either. But he appreciated the imagination of the seven year old girl who wrote about herself going through a mirror to become a boy with whom this Cinderella fell in love.

'A long time ago there were monsters in Halloween. The monsters smashed the boxes in the shops. They killed people . . . . I saw a dragon sword in a rock. I

pulled it out. A dragon flew out from the sword . . . .
lived happily ever after with the dragon.' Long couldn't
understand what Halloween was, but from the illustration, he
could figure out what monsters were and how the boy fought
them with the help of the dragon.

There were also stories of a talking pillow, of a crazy fairy
who liked others to shout at her, of a naughty princess who
failed in the 'spelling test', of a girl going to someone called
'Santa Claus', of a pair of jumping 'trainers' that could take you
to 'Africa', of a butterfly that could turn everything new and
more beautiful, of a diamond inside a frog . . . .

It was the first time Long had listened to stories from
children. The teacher told him they were primary one to
primary three students. He assumed this was referring to
their study levels. But anyway he could tell they were only
children aged from six to eight. Long couldn't recall what he
himself had in mind at such an age but he was sure he didn't
make up any stories. In his world, children had no reason to
create stories except for telling lies. Stories were told by adults
to children to tell them the origins of the different sayings.
There were also the traditional myths and legends passed on
from generation to generation. Long could still remember
those stories his mother told him when he was a child. He
had pictured in his mind those characters like Pangu, Nuwa,
the Jade Emperor and other heavenly immortals, the cowherd
and the spinning girl . . . But not even once had he thought
of actually drawing them. But now, the students' illustrations
and the many picture books in the class book corner were
inspiring him to try the idea. Of course, it'd be just for fun
and for the eyes of his animal friends only. People of his time

would not appreciate such things. This was Long's thought at that moment but who knew what would happen next?

Since Zoe had introduced Long to the teacher and her classmates as someone working with her dad at the same magazine, they were all taking him as a substitute lecturer for that lesson. Once the sharing session of stories from the previous week was over, students began putting up their hands. As usual, they didn't actually wait for their turns and questions were being fired at the same time the pupils were raising their hands.

'Mr. K.K., what story are you going to read to us?'

'Errrh . . . let me see . . .' Long was looking to Zoe for help.

'Do we need to write a new story today?'

'Errrh . . . , I think so . . . .' Again, Long looked at Zoe, who was nodding to agree.

'What about the Little Author Project? How's it going?'

Finally, there was something he could answer. 'We are told to go ahead with it.'

'That's good news. So class, let's take a break first. Five minutes for toilet and water.' The teacher announced.

It was good news for Long. He could take a break and ask Zoe for help. But no, the teacher was approaching. The teacher gave the students a break so she could discuss with Long to see if there was any change to the lesson plan that she had worked out with Gavin. 'So are we following the plan and we'll start the co-writing of a story for the project?'

'Yes, sure.' Long was glad there was a plan but the relaxed feeling couldn't last for even ten seconds.

'So, have you thought of the main plot of the story?'

'Me?'

'Errrh . . . Or did Gavin leave you his idea?'

'Hey, I have an idea!' Gavin suddenly sprang up from among the bull-eyed daisies. The fairies lingering with him were glad to see a smile on their visitor's face again. They paused in whatever they were doing to wait for Gavin's idea.

Gavin drew a small circle in the air with his finger. 'I'm too big to go through this hole but you're not. I can draw a small doorway with the feather and one of you can . . . .' Before Gavin could finish, the fairies were already discussing things among themselves.

'We can't go to the human world. The queen won't let us go'. The brave Alyssa's direct response put water on Gavin's spark of an idea. If this was not enough to extinguish the fire, the questions and worries of the others certainly did.

'Especially your world. We know nothing about it.'

'Is there a garden there? We would not survive without flowers.'

'What if the hole you draw doesn't lead us to your world but somewhere else?'

'How are we going to return?'

'What do you want us to do in your world?' Periwinkle appeared quite interested to know the plan.

'Forget about it! I am sorry I hadn't been thoughtful enough to see things from your point of view.' Gavin realized that he had made an impulsive suggestion, a self-centered decision, once again, a plan that put others at risk. He was ready to drop the idea but Periwinkle was not.

'I'll go. Just tell me what you want me to do once I get to your world.' Periwinkle was determined to help even though she was well aware of the danger. She had done the same thing for Princess Mariana in Gavin's story. She was brave.

She was altruistic. She was strong willed. Gavin had created her with such personality features in that story. But he didn't feel he should take advantage of that now.

'No. They're right. How can I be sure that the other side of the portal will be the world I came from? Even if it is the same world, how can I be sure you will arrive safely at my home?'

'Trust your magic feather. It does what you will. Just focus and picture the right place.'

'But my world is really different from here. It's not even like the world where Princess Mariana lived.'

'Don't worry about me! I'm a fairy. Of course, I have tricks to survive different environments and protect myself from dangers.'

'But I can't draw a doorway from here for you to return.'

'I know. But when you are back in your world, you will send me home. You must already have in mind a solution for the problem of how we can help you to get home, right?'

'My fate depends on Long now. He's the only one that can draw with that feather. My plan is to ask one of you to pass him this message so that he'll come again in his dream and draw the doorway for me.'

'You're assuming humans can control their dreams.' Alyssa pointed out the problem at once. She was right and Gavin should have realized it. He'd wished for and tried every night to get to Fairyland in his dream. If that had worked, he wouldn't have needed that magic feather.

'Why don't you just throw a note and the feather across? Your friend could come if he had the feather.' The clever Cloris made a more thoughtful suggestion and received applause from the rest.

Gavin had thought of that. But he had no confidence that Long considered him a friend or that he would come to save him once he got back the feather. Besides, there could be other accidents. 'Long may not see the note or the feather. It's too risky to leave the feather by itself because we could lose our only key forever.'

'If Periwinkle's going, then just let her take the feather with her. At least that ensures your friend can come across and Periwinkle can return.'

'It may be too heavy for me to carry it alone.' Obviously, the feather was really too big for Periwinkle but she knew she could manage it if she had to. Periwinkle was just finding a good excuse for Gavin because she could understand his feelings of insecurity about parting with the feather.

'But then we still have the problem of how to make sure your friend can come here through his dream.' The fairy boy Crisento reminded them.

Silence fell again as no one had any better suggestion. Just then they could see their Queen approaching. She had come to check how things were going on with Gavin. Somehow the Queen did know more than the others. She could keep the secret but she disclosed it to offer Gavin a chance. 'Remember the witch who grows all kinds of herbs in her garden . . . .'

Of course, Gavin hadn't forgotten about her since he believed she was one of his creations as well. The Queen continued as if she could read Gavin's mind, 'Yes, it's the witch you'd mentioned in your story and from whom Princess Mariana had got the herb to save her lover. She grows all kinds of magical plants, among which is the herb called Dreamosemary. It can induce people to dream the people or the place they wish for.'

'Dreamosemary!' So this is the secret key to enter Fairyland. Gavin couldn't withhold his excitement.

'Now you know the secret. I can't stop you from thinking of other ways you might use it but I trust you not to abuse your knowledge or to let the secret spread.' In fact, the Queen wasn't too worried. Even if humans knew how to dream of Fairyland, it wouldn't be easy to get the herb from the witch.

'Your majesty, may I ask for your permission to go with Gavin to look for the witch?' Periwinkle was determined to take Gavin to the 'human world' through the secret passageway that she had discovered. That was the passage under the rose bushes through which she'd brought Mariana back to her world.

'Yes, he will need your help. It will be quite an adventure for him.'

'Let's write an adventurous story.' The girl with a pony tail was the first to suggest the idea. Her name was Cindy.

'Yes, I can kill the monsters.' Norman was the boy with sticking out front teeth.

'No you can't. The monsters will eat you.' The girl with short hair who always argued with Norman was called Ada.

'We need the fairies to help us.' Priscilla was the girl in the pink dress, sitting next to Zoe.

'But I have a special sword.' Andy was a chubby boy with a front tooth missing.

'Me, too. My sword has superpower light.' Tommy was the one with a pair of framed ovals just in front of his eyes. Long noticed that many people in this world were wearing such things and later he found out that they were called spectacles.

'But it was just a toothpick for the giant.' Zoe joined in the argument.

'. . . . .'

The teacher kept calling names and more children made their suggestions, projecting themselves in the different circumstances.

Five minutes ago, Long had still been worrying as he felt his mind totally blank. Now he was much inspired by these expressive and imaginative boys and girls. An adventurous story—it was quite an interesting idea for Long. He himself was undergoing an adventure in this new world. All those monsters, good or bad, that he had met during his half an hour journey to school were quite enough excitement for him. He was happy to be in safe room just discussing the idea with children now. What kinds of adventure would Gavin undergo in his fairy world?

Long had an idea. *How would such a self-centred, arrogant man who made up stories to manipulate lives in other worlds, himself face the challenges in an imaginary world.*

'Boys and girls, thank you for all your ideas. They are great and we can now put them together to make up our adventurous fairy tale for the little authors' project.' The teacher looked at Long for something conclusive.

Long was prepared to say his part. 'The main character is an author. He's curious to know what the story world is like. One day, he finds a magic doorway and he steps across but he can't find his way back.'

'Does the author have a name?' Andy asked.

'Gavin.'

'Mr. Gavin.' Noises and laughter arose as the class found it very exciting to imagine their mentor in the story.

'Is it Zoe's daddy, our Mr. Gavin? He's an author also.' Ada was trying to confirm her connection.

'Yes, will that be more interesting?' Long proposed it tentatively because he was also concerned about Zoe's feelings. He looked at Zoe but she was very excited too.

'Yes, my daddy would like to go to the story world. That may help him to find new ideas. Can I go with him? I know he will take me with him.'

'Can I go too? I'm very good at fighting monsters.' Norman was the first to ask Zoe and the others soon followed. Long was surprised by their reactions. It seemed that they were all looking forward to such a trip.

'No, no children can go. It's very dangerous and we must make the story dangerous and exciting, right? Gavin has to face the challenges all by himself. He will meet monsters, giants, witches, pirates, ghosts, serpents, . . . what else?.' Long felt happy just to repeat those dangerous characters mentioned by the kids and to imagine Gavin's fear in meeting them.

'But he can also meet a good fairy or a wise wizard.'

'Make new friends.'

'See the unicorn.'

'Find the treasure.'

'Gain magical power.'

'Get a powerful sword.'

'Save a princess.'

'. . . . .'

After all, kids tend to be positive with fairy tales. Should Long feel grateful that he was from a fairy tale and not a tragedy? Or should Gavin feel lucky now that Long was inspired to write an adventurous fairy tale and not a thriller or ghost story?

'Let's begin the story . . . .'

'Once upon a time, there was a writer called Gavin.' Norman made the customary beginning. Long wrote it down.

'He was very good at writing fairy tales for children. He was brave, kind and clever.' Zoe added a good description of the character. Long didn't agree but still he wrote the lines down.

'Let's think of how he got inside the fairy world.' Long was eager to go directly to Gavin meeting all sorts of dangers.

'Through a mirror.' Melissa was the girl who wrote herself through a mirror to become a boy.

'No, people will think we copied from Alice in wonderland.'

'Ah! I know when Gavin was watching *Transformer*, the monsters came out and grabbed him in . . . .' Long could tell that this boy called Andy spent long hours in front of the T.V.

'No, my dad doesn't like watching those cartoons.'

'When he was taking a bath, he was washed down the drain . . .'

'Then he will have no clothes to wear . . .'

'Where's Mr. Gavin right now?' Ada asked seriously.

'He may be in the forest now, doing research.' Zoe prayed that he was safe from the wild beasts.

'Then let him walk into the dark forest. It was getting darker and darker and when he came out of the forest, he was in the fairy world.' Ada was telling the story as if it had already happened. That bothered Zoe.

'No . . . .' Zoe was the only one against; most of the others were chorusing approval.

'That's good.'
'Good idea.'
'Yes, I agree.'
'Okay, let it happen this way!'

15

I can't believe that we are doing such a thing

Gavin followed Periwinkle through the winding path in the field of flowers. After countless turns, the scent of the roses became more and more distinguishable from that of the other blooms. Extending along the horizon, the first roses of Fairyland came into view. Gavin couldn't help speeding up his pace. Not long after seeing the first of them, he was found himself amid an endless field of different kinds and colours of roses. Not a single blossom of another flower type could now be spotted.

'This is the boundary, beyond which is the human world. Keep close to me or you will get lost in the maze.'

Gavin followed Periwinkle through the rose bushes, turning one way or another, here and there. Anyone watching from above would soon have seen them disappear. As they moved forward, Gavin had the feeling they were shrinking since the bushes ahead of them were getting taller and taller. The path was getting dimmer and cooler as the final sun ray could no longer penetrate through the thick bushes. Soon Gavin was not sure if he was under the bushes or under the ground. Now complete darkness fell upon him.

It was the first time that Gavin had travelled with no light at all. Periwinkle was singing so Gavin could follow. It was one of the fairy songs that Gavin knew so he could sing along. But as Gavin could hear the trembling in his voice, he stopped to avoid showing his fear. To calm himself, he tried to recall the experience of night walks when he was in the boys scouts. It was almost thirty years ago. There was usually at least some moonlight so that after the first few minutes of adapting to the dark, he could use his night vision. He was less scared then or it was such a long time ago that he had forgotten the fear. When his mind drifted back from the pretend howling and laughter of his young friends back to the complete silence of the present moment, Gavin was really scared.

Then he realized he couldn't hear Periwinkle's voice anymore. When did she stop singing? Was he moving so slowly that he was too far behind or had he made a wrong turn so that he was not even on the same track as her? He called out to Periwinkle but could only hear his own echo. That frightened him further. Should he stop or move on faster or make a 180 degree turn to hopefully return on the same path back to where he could still see some light?

'. . . . Gavin was walking in the dark by himself. He felt himself lost and he was scared. It seemed that he was moving through a dark tunnel all by himself. Finally, he could see some light ahead. He was so excited that he ran as fast as his legs could carry him. He was running too fast to halt quickly when he saw something lying just a step in front of him. He tripped and fell onto that bumpy thing. Gavin tried to get up but before he could stand straight, he could feel that bumpy thing moving and the next moment, he was thrown up in the air and fell hard on rocky ground . . . .'

Zoe was reading aloud the draft that was created by the class. She put down the draft, ate a couple of French fries, took a big gulp of milk shake and then turned to Long who was busy drawing a bumpy dragon on the napkins.

'I can't believe that we are doing such a thing to my dad. It must hurt.'

'It's just a story. He will appreciate our imagination when he reads it.' Long put down the pen and closed the dragon book that Tommy had lent him.

Long took another big bite of his delicious bun. Two days ago, he would never have imagined himself eating and enjoying eating such a bun called Big Mac. He would never have imagined that a dragon was not long like a snake. He would never have imagined that he was actually quite imaginative. Of course up to the present moment, it was also beyond Long's imagination or anybody's that things they wrote and drew actually happened to Gavin in the other world.

Gavin could feel the heat of fire breathing out from the dragon's mouth, just a few inches away from his face. Within that instant while the dragon leant back his head ready for a second blast, Gavin crawled up and tried to run as fast as he could. Gavin could feel his back muscles aching because of the heavy fall just a moment ago. He would have had to lie in bed for a few days and to massage his back with ointments to relieve the pain and bruises. But now the pain couldn't even slow him down. He was running for his life.

The dragon didn't move but just kept growling behind Gavin, pressing him to keep running and tire himself out.

Gavin ran and ran until he was among some trees. Even though the trees were not too tall, he wished they might help to block the dragon's view and discourage the creature from following him. Just when he began to slow down, he felt the wind and heard the flapping. Before he could look up, the dragon was flying down right in front of him among the shower of pink petals from the blossoms of the trees. It lowered its head and snarled, with the fire blowing close to Gavin's face. The monster had not intended to kill its prey in one move. Gavin turned to run in the other direction. He ran and ran until his aching legs couldn't support him any further. He was slowing down, panting. This time, the dragon didn't even fly. It just took two easy steps backward and was right behind him. Gavin knew his chance to escape was small but he couldn't let himself die here. Despite the pain in his legs, he tried to run again. But a sudden cramp made him fall. Gavin was now crawling for his life.

Gavin thought he should have had given up from the moment the dragon threw him up in the air. He believed he had never been a truly persevering person. In his younger days, he had never given up pursuing his dream to be a great surgeon because he had never met real difficulty. He was really good in his studies and surgery skills. If he had failed in one of his exams, would he have given up earlier? He couldn't tell but he had left his career five years ago. He knew that he could still save lives even though he was not able to save his beloved. Why had he given up? Gavin had believed that perseverance couldn't help in hopeless circumstances. He had seen Sofia insisting and struggling till the last moment but the result remained unavoidably unchanged. And now, now he should give up trying to escape. Why suffer more than necessary now that the end was near. But he didn't give up. The thought of Zoe had made him struggle on, even now that he could only crawl for his life.

The dragon was ahead of him. It lowered its head and was face to face with Gavin. It was opening its mouth. Gavin closed his eyes. It was a yucky smell and next he could feel some wet and slimy fluid dropping onto him. The dragon had opened its mouth to lick him and wrapped him up in its slimy saliva. It was only then that Gavin noticed that the dragon had two necks and two heads.

"It was then that Gavin noticed the dragon has two necks and two heads."

Long passed another napkin to Zoe showing her the finished illustration of the double headed dragon and her dad wrapped in slime. Zoe did her job of adding some spikes on one of the heads. She touched her dad in the picture as if she could clean up the slime from his face. 'It was so yuck! Only that yucky Norman could think of such yucky thing.'

'But it was quite interesting.' *In fact all the kids seemed very amused with that idea. All kids like awful things?* While Long was still considering the question, his assumption was further supported.

'Let's colour the slime pink' Zoe was dripping some strawberry milkshake on her hand to show Long the pink slime.

'You are the yuckiest!'

'Oh . . . Yeah! And I have drunk a whole cup of pink slime.'

Long couldn't help laughing. Zoe found it very funny and she laughed also. She made further funny faces that made Long laugh and laugh. It seemed to be the first time in his life that he was laughing so heartily. His childhood was short if he'd had one. He shared his mum's workload since a very young age, collecting wood on the hills, carrying water over a long distance, washing the clothes down the river . . . He did have a happy time with his mum but no crazy moments. His friends were of similar background so everyone was quite mature and had to devote most of the time taking care of the family. They didn't have the leisure for these silly jokes and fun. Long was grateful to have met Zoe.

'I think we better add some lines saying that daddy would wash himself at a river or waterfall or something like that.'

'It's just a story. Do you think your dad will come home soaked in slime?'

'But because you draw it so real. I can't help picturing it and smelling it.' Zoe was appreciating the illustrations Long had drawn for the story. She laid out the pictured napkins on the table in sequence. It was liked a comics. As Long was adding some peach blossoms and other plants in the background, Zoe continued to read the draft.

'Where was I up to?'

'about the dragon throwing Gavin hard on the rocky ground.'

'Ah . . . yes . . . . Let me continue. Gavin got up and tried to run as fast as he could. The double-headed dragon flew and caught up with him easily. Its angry head with spikes blew fire to scare him. Gavin ran away until he was too tired to run anymore. This time the good head was coming down to Gavin but it did not breathe fire on him. It licked him and covered him with slimy saliva. When the spiky head blew fire on Gavin again . . .'

Gavin could distinguish the two heads now. It was a double headed dragon. The one with spikes was turning to him also. Before Gavin could react, a blast of dazzling hot fire was blowing onto him. Gavin thought he would be burnt but the fire went out almost at once. The yucky slime had protected him from the flames.

Gavin could see now that the spiky head was trying to kill him while the other head, a spotty head, was trying to save him. The friendly head took Gavin up in its mouth and put him on its long neck. But that didn't stop the spiky head's attack. The dragon's body was moving in a ridiculous way since both heads were trying to command it to move in such a way to match their intended acts. The two heads kept swinging from side to side. The spiky head was trying to bite Gavin because it could not use its fire on the other head. If it did so it would also feel the pain. Gavin knew that he would either be trodden to death or torn to shreds once he fell. He was trying to hold on tight but that wasn't easy. He was exhausted from his run and the wild swinging of the neck he was riding made him dizzy. Worse still, the slime made it too slippery to keep a proper grip. Finally Gavin fell but the friendly head was quick to pick him up and kept him safely gripped between its teeth.

So Gavin was held swinging upside down. That roller coaster move made him sick, he screamed and threw up. Still, in a while he found himself adjusting as his mind became occupied. He had written stories about good and bad dragons before. He just couldn't imagine that he would meet both—in the one dragon's body—in his real life. *Wait, is it real? Am I real?* He knew he was no brave knight but he just hoped that he would be as lucky as most protagonists in stories. Was Gavin having these odd thoughts merely because the swinging upside down was affecting his brain or was it just because there was nothing else he could physically do? Picturing himself as a knight fighting a bad dragon with a sword made it easier to tolerate the pains and violent motions now. Imagining himself in a story world made him feel he had a better chance to survive.

It was a long fight of hours in the story world but the version of Zoe and her friends consisted of just a few lines.

' . . . The evil head was trying to get Gavin while the good head was trying to protect him. The two heads fought with each other until they were both too tired to go on. Gavin took out a sword and cut off the evil head. Finally he became friends with the single headed dragon. The end.'

'Where did Gavin find a sword?' Long asked since he had not drawn any sword for him so far.'

'Yes, a good question. Why hadn't we noticed it in the class before? But anyway, I don't like the ending too much. Let's make some changes.'

'Are you okay?' Periwinkle was hovering upside down in front of Gavin's eyes.

'You! Yes, of course! Where have you been? But I must be imagining you.' Still, Gavin felt more optimistic now.

'But I am here. You're not imagining me.'

'You are here? Since when?'

'Since we came out from the dark tunnel. You were just too busy to notice me.'

The moon began to rise and the dragon was so tired that it began to lie down. Not long after that, snores came from the evil head. It had fallen asleep. The good head had put Gavin down, and to regain some strength, he began eating the surrounding plants.

Gavin, still in a confused state, was trying to recall what had happened. 'I lost you, didn't I? I felt I was all by myself in the dark tunnel. I just moved on blindly until I saw the light and I ran out and tripped over the dragon. It tried . . . , well, part of it tried to attack me and the other head . . . .'

'I know. I saw it. I told you I was here. The dragon was moving this way and that, flying up and down. The heads were swinging around so much I was almost hit.'

'Then how come I didn't see you?'

'Perhaps you were too busy to notice me. I'm small so maybe I just became part of the background. Sometimes things are like that. We miss things that are in front of us. We come across things we've never expected.'

The dragon was unexpected. And how could Gavin have guessed what was going to happen next?

Gavin could hear the dragon whispering to him now. 'You must be the brave knight come to save me.'

'No, I am not a knight. I was just imagining just now.' *But the dragon couldn't have known that.*

'I've been waiting for years and I can feel that you're the knight who's come to help.'

'No, I'm not but I will try my best to help if I am able to.'

The spiky head stopped snoring and was turning from one side to another. Eyes fixed on it, Gavin and the friendly head just kept still and quiet. They were afraid to wake the bad head. Sensing the danger, Periwinkle was quick to act. From the moon ray, she could collect the sleeping dust and she sprinkled a pinch of it on the spiky head. That made it snore again.

Feeling that it was sound asleep, the good part of the dragon stood its shared body up gently with the sleeping head supported on the neck of the friendly head. Now the good head asked Gavin to climb on its back and it lifted off. Periwinkle caught up to sit on Gavin's shoulder. After a short flight, the dragon began to head down, towards the cliff. They descended so fast, Gavin thought they were going to crash. But with a twist, he found they were already down through a chasm just big enough for them. They flew down with the moonlight to a hidden cave. That was the dragon's lair. Under the moonlight, they could see a big piece of rock right in the centre. A few inches above it was something glittering in the air. It was a sapphire reflecting the moon's rays. As Gavin and Periwinkle moved closer, they could see that it was not suspended in the air but embedded on a cross. No, it was not a cross. It was the hilt of a sword, the blade of which was buried in the rock.

'If you can pull it out, then you're the one I am waiting for.'

'No way, you're kidding. I am not King Arthur and I don't even believe in that stuff. It was just a legend.'

'If so, then why don't you try to disprove it?'

'Okay. I'll try but just don't expect too much from me.'

The friendly head nodded.

Gavin stepped forward and with both hands on the hilt, he pulled as hard as he could. It didn't move at all. Seeing the disappointment on the dragon's face, Gavin tried again though he hadn't the least belief that he could work the miracle required. As he expected, nothing budged.

'Maybe you should try one more time by imagining that you can do it. Maybe if you believe you can do it . . .' Periwinkle suggested.

'Will it make a difference?' But what was there to lose. So Gavin decided to try. Gavin closed his eyes and pictured himself in shining armour again. He was now a brave knight going to help the dragon retrieve a precious sword. It wasn't that hard. It had once been his childhood fantasy. Slowly he slid his hand on the hilt, with the thumb rubbing the sapphire to get the best grip. Sir Gavin pulled and as his arms moved up, he could feel the sword coming up with them.

Periwinkle cheered. The dragon was moved to tears. And Gavin was shocked by what had happened. 'So it worked . . .'he muttered and before Gavin could get over the shock, the dragon was down on its knees pleading for help.

'Thank you very much. Now would you please take the sword and cut the other head off my body?'

'What? Why? I thought you just needed me to get the sword for you. I can't kill you.'

'No, it won't kill me. You just need to cut that evil head off.'

16

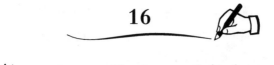

*He might really have skilful hands
and a kind heart*

When the spiky head fell asleep, the dragon took Gavin to a cave. It showed Gavin a shiny sword half buried inside a rock. It asked Gavin to get it out and cut the evil head off.' Zoe was reading aloud as she kept writing.

'This was a good idea and then . . .' Long was appreciative.

'Then it's time to go. Remember we need to go to the movie.'

Zoe was quick to pack the things after Long drew a last picture of Gavin trying hard to pull out the sword.

'Could he get the sword out?'

'Of course! Let's go.'

'But how could he do it?'

'It's a story. He can do anything.'

'Why did the dragon have to ask Gavin to help?'

' . . . because he was brave.'

'Why he would help?'

' . . . because he was kind.'

Long didn't agree but he knew what Zoe would say. *It's a story.*

It's a story. Long had met a goddess before but after all he was still a rational person. On their way to the cinema, Long was still puzzled by these kinds of questions. 'Why did the dragon have two heads?'

'We don't need to know.' The two-headedness of dragons was not a question to a child and especially not to an imaginative child like Zoe.

'Please cut my head off!' The dragon kept begging.

But it's part of you.'

'No, it wasn't before.'

'So what had happened?'

'It's a long story. I was the dragon of the dark wizard. He was the courtier of King Damocles and I helped to guard his dungeon. Then there was a time, I was touched by the beautiful voice of a nightingale locked in the dungeon. She was the runaway bride of the ruthless king. The wizard turned her into a bird under the king's command. Night after night, I heard her beautiful singing and that softened my heart.'

As the dragon was telling his story, Gavin was recalling one of his stories. *She was called Nysis. Her singing could tame the lions and stop the storm. Her lover was called Dion. He was the best blacksmith in the kingdom. He could make a dagger that would pierce the heart of the immortal serpent, a cutlass that could open the sea, an axe that would take off a giant's arm . . . One night, Dion came to the dungeon with a sword that could cut open the wizard's invisible cage, in which the nightingale was trapped.*

'I could have stopped them but I let them go. The man gave me this sword. Yes the one you are holding now though not with the sapphire yet. King Damocles was very angry and commanded the wizard to kill me, but the wizard didn't. He gave my sword to the king with the lie that I had been just too foolish to think that the king would like the sword more than the bride. And actually he did prefer the sword. So my life was spared. The king took possession of the sword and that's how it got the sapphire.'

Gavin was sure it was the story he'd written but his story ended when the king took the sword and agreed to let the couple flee. He didn't even know that the king had added a sapphire to it. He signaled the dragon to go on with his story as he ran his fingers gently along the surface of the sword with a special affection.

'The dark wizard knew that I had a kind heart so he cast a spell on me to bring this evil head out from my body. He sent me away as a punishment for betraying him. Then after some years, the king died. After his death, the wizard took the sword and fixed it in this rock. Through secret signs, he let me know that this sword was the only weapon that could break his spell. Actually he had a kind heart, too. From that time until this, I was guarding the sword and waiting for the man who could pull it out and free me from the spell. And finally you came.'

Gavin was caught in his thought. He knew the story or at least part of it. In his story, the dragon was just a side character. He didn't know that behind his romantic fairy tale of 'The Blacksmith and the Nightingale', the dragon that once helped the couple had such a fate. He had never expected that he would be holding the sword he made up in his story. He had never imagined the fate of his character was now relying on his hands. How could he reject to help?

But Gavin was sometimes quite realistic. He didn't know how far the fairy tale will go. So to play safe, he asked Periwinkle to try getting him something he needed.

'I need all the money!' Zoe was urging Long to take out all the coins as they walked by the donation counter in the shopping mall. It was of an organization called "Medecins Sans Frontiers". She put every single one into a transparent box.

Zoe felt very contented after making the donation and the volunteers showed their appreciation of her deed with smiles. Long felt proud of her also after he had read the leaflet about the organization. 'You have a very kind heart.'

'My daddy, too. He mails a cheque to them every month. But every time when we see some institutions' donation counters or flag sales for charity, he will ask me to put some change in their boxes. That's why we have brought all those coins.'

After his last argument with Gavin, Long found it hard to imagine this man being as kind hearted as his daughter said. 'He doesn't seem so charitable to me.'

'Why do you say that?' Zoe was upset to hear Long's comment.

Long regretted his slip of the tongue. Even though he was still angry with Gavin, he shouldn't have spoken about him negatively in front of his daughter. 'No, I meant, I didn't know about that.

'Ah! Of course, he doesn't want to let others know. And do you know why he particularly likes the MSF? He's not just a regular donor. He had thought of joining them to help the sick in those African countries. Granny told me that.'

Zoe was happy again when she talked about her dad. And she kept talking about him. 'Do you know that my dad was a doctor before? He was a great surgeon. That was before my mummy got sick. He cured a lot of people. He saved lives.'

'Er . . . hhh. I think he's better suited to being a writer.' Long said that not because he appreciated his writing. In his case, how would a character judge his creator objectively? But Long just could not accept the idea of a selfish and arrogant man like Gavin being a great doctor. Not even an ordinary doctor.

'Of course, he had the talent to be a great writer also. But Granny said that he had loved the idea of being a doctor since he was small. He cared about his patients and he had a good reputation in the hospital where he worked. Granny felt it a pity that he quit the job.'

'Hi, Zoe.' A middle-aged lady called out from a bakery as Zoe and Long were walking by it.

'Hi, Mrs. Lam.' It was too late to pretend not to see her so Zoe went into the shop with Long.

'Where's Dr. Au?'

'He's at the conference, in Shanghai. This is his friend, KK. He works for the magazine too . . .'

The lady nodded at Long but she was concerned about Gavin. 'A medical conference?'

'No, for writers.'

'Oh! . . .' Obviously, the lady was quite disappointed. 'It's because for the first time in all these years, I see him leaving you behind. So I thought he's ready to be a doctor again . . . . Don't misunderstand me. I don't mean it's because of you . . . .'

'It's okay. I understand.' Zoe had heard that kind of slip of the tongue before. She pulled Long's sleeve to ask him to leave.

But the lady had already grasped Long's other arm and was talking to him. 'I like his stories also but I still feel a bit of a pity. He's the best doctor I ever met. If it was not for Dr. Au, my son would have died in that accident. No other doctors dared to take the bullet out from his skull. Of course, my son didn't deserve to be saved. He was the one who shot the police officer. Only Dr. Au didn't view him as a robber. He treated him with the same care as he would give any patient in danger. Dr. Au saved his life. You won't understand. That night in the emergency room I could see the attitudes of the other doctors, nurses and the police. Of course, I don't blame them. My son deserved that but . . . .

'Excuse me, Mrs. Lam. But we're in a hurry for the movie.' Zoe had to interrupt or her speech would never end.

'Take the muffins then. Take them or I won't be happy.' The lady insisted.

So Zoe took the bag or else she wouldn't let them go. 'I'll tell my daddy about your kindness.'

'We have been talking and talking, that's why I forgot I should bypass the bakery.' Zoe felt more relaxed once they turned the corner and Mrs. Lam was out of sight.

'But what she said was true?'

'Yes, I have heard that story many times already. Mrs. Lam's son is still in jail. My daddy said he was glad to have saved that young man's life. He was sure when someone is given a second chance he won't waste it. And my daddy is right. Last time, Mrs. Lam told us that his son has passed the A-Level in jail. A-Level is our public exam. He's even determined to be a doctor.'

To be fair, Long felt the need to adjust his impression for Gavin. *Gavin was self-centred and arrogant but at least he might really have skilful hands and a kind heart.*

Periwinkle had all the things ready for Gavin. She had flown around to collect some detached spikes from the porcupines for him and some threads of flax fibre. Periwinkle sprinkled more sleeping dust on the dragon. Gavin washed his hands thoroughly in one of the underground pools. He was ready.

Gavin knew he was the right person to do the job. He was a surgeon. He knew how to amputate. Instead of a scalpel, with one blow of the sharp sword, he cut off the spiky head. There was not much bleeding but still he sutured the wound up carefully with the spike and thread. He was quite confident with his skill that when the wound healed, there wouldn't be any scar.

While Zoe was waiting for the pop corn, Long grasped a napkin from the tuck shop and took out his pen. When Zoe handed him the pop corn, he had finished drawing a new picture for the story. In the picture, Gavin was suturing the wound of the dragon under the gentle moonlight.

Before the operation, Gavin hadn't thought of why he was inspired to work it out this way. It was supposed to be fairy tale stuff and things would go fine just by magic. But now he was glad he had done it this way. It gave him the pleasure that he had long missed. He missed the contentment of a perfect cut and a perfect suture. He missed the satisfaction of saving life, curing the sick and healing the injured. At this moment, the first moment in these five years, he felt the desire to return to the profession. More than the desire, he felt the confidence. And above all, he had the heart again.

17

I believe it could have happened

Gavin slept soundly that night, partly because of the physical exhaustion and partly because of the psychological contentment. But he woke up early the next morning because he couldn't afford any leisure or further rest. He had to find the witch as soon as possible.

'If we keep going east, over those mountains, we might possibly find Princess Mariana's castle. She should be able to lead us to the witch.' Periwinkle was optimistic.

'I'll go with you. These few years I keep hearing news about that kingdom with gold on the trees and silver in the sea. I've long desired to pay it a visit. But since I was afraid that my evil head would do harm to the people there, I tried to suppress thinking about it. Now finally I'm free to go.' Actually the dragon also wished to accompany them for protection and to give them a lift.

As they were ascending, Gavin recalled the picture he had in mind when he was a child. It was just a snap shot of a young boy flying proudly on the back of his pet dragon. He couldn't recall much detail. He wasn't even sure the young boy had his face. But somehow he knew it was him in his favourite Robokon T-shirt. That dream had faded away.

Now as a man of almost forty, having long passed the age to believe in fantasy, here he was flying on a real dragon. Better than expected, he even had a sword on his lap. All these years that he was a creator of fantasy, he couldn't persuade himself that a fairy tale world could be true, even though he wished it were so. Now he was in such a world but who had created it?

Flying above the hills, Gavin thought it worth all those fights and pains in having met the dragon. How would he be able to walk all this distance to the other side of the mountains? His legs were aching just thinking of it. When he got home, he should really start taking more exercise. Maybe he could ask Zoe to go with him jogging every evening. Or he should learn cycling or enroll in an ice-skating beginner course so he could join Zoe for her favourite activities. A moment ago he was still fascinated by the new experience. Now the thought of Zoe made him regret the adventure. Zoe must be worrying about him right now.

'Ah! . . .' Zoe almost screamed together with the characters in the movie and so did Long. They felt their hearts bursting and going down with the characters into an abyss that led all the way to the centre of Earth. Zoe took a big gulp of the soda.

It was the first time Long had watched a whole movie. When the advertisements were still showing Long thought it was something like what he had watched in Gavin's home but just much, much bigger. But then when the movie started and he did what Zoe did, putting in front of his eyes that thing called 3D spectacles, Long found himself being taken on a new adventure. Things became as real as if they were just happening right in front of him. As a reflex, he moved sideways to avoid the water spat out by the hero in the movie. More than once, he couldn't resist stretching out his hand to touch or catch the things before him. 'Just keep eating the popcorn and drink the soda. It reminds you that you're not inside the movie.' That was Zoe's advice to Long and it helped for a while.

But when the movie got to its climax, Long felt his heart beating as fast as the characters' when he experienced every close shave with them. And it was the same for Zoe. She was holding onto Long, tensing up, screaming and sighing with him. Who would still remember to eat the popcorn when they were on such an adventure?

On their way home, Zoe was still recalling and talking excitedly about the movie. She had watched similar 3D shows at Disney Land but the impression from cartoons was no match for real persons. Despite knowing that the movie wasn't real, the feeling was.

Long was definitely unprepared for such an adventure. Coming to Gavin's study the day before happened all within less than a minute. But just now, within that one and a half hours, he felt he was being taken on another trip with the characters, having shared their experience and relieved by now to have returned intact. Long wouldn't mind if his own trip took longer than a movie. He just wished that he would finally return to his own world just like when the movie was over.

' . . . I wish daddy was with us. He liked the original story. He read that book to me before.'

'It was a written story?'

'Yes, "Journey to the centre of the Earth" by Jules Verne". But the setting of the movie changed. The original story happened in the past.'

'It actually happened?'

'No, of course not. I meant the story was set over a hundred years ago.' At first, Zoe found Long's question quite silly but then she had to admit that sometimes she asked the same question with other stories. So she added, 'But I believe it could have happened.'

Neither Zoe's negative answer nor her belief had played any role in what Long was thinking at that moment. The seed of belief was there and it had just begun to sprout when those words came spontaneously out of his mouth. If my life happened to be exactly like something written, could it be possible that other written stories might have happened somewhere in time? Long couldn't help wondering. The thing had its own logic. If my story developed as it was written, then was what we've been writing actually happening to Gavin, somewhere, sometime, maybe right now? It wasn't that Long wished for such a thing but he couldn't understand why, instead of feeling disappointed, it made him feel excited. He wanted to get back to Gavin's story straight away.

Once they were home, Long didn't waste a minute on any other business. He immersed himself in the rich resources of fairy tales, picture story books and comics in Gavin's study. He was looking for further inspiration through the images, particularly some scary features—the wicked witch, the man-eating ogre, the dark wood, the gingerbread house. Long was determined to make Gavin go through hardships and dangers to observe his cowardice and incapability in the story world. He wasn't sure Gavin would actually experience what they wrote but just the thought of that possibility was sufficient to satisfy him. But then what if Gavin would really get killed or hurt? Long hesitated.

Zoe was sure of what has to be written. Inspired by the movie, Zoe was as enthusiastic as Long to continue writing the story about her dad. She was expecting her father figure to get through the adventures with his courage and wit like the hero of the movie they'd just seen. But her hero didn't go down into the earth, he went up into the sky.

Zoe began writing, 'The next morning, the dragon carried Gavin on his back and they were flying over high mountains. They'd been airborne for some time when they saw a white . . .

On the dragon's back, Gavin could see a shiny white spot against a green background. It became more and more distinct as they flew lower and approached closer. Except for the lake, the whole slope was basically green with pastures, crops and vast areas of orchards. On the cliff was a white castle, flanked by a moat on the three sides not facing the sea. The castle was well built with concentric walls of white granite. The bailey was roughly hexagonal and there was a square tower at each corner. The four storey keep was magnificent, pearly white and gleaming under the sun. Yet it appeared a bit odd to Gavin. There was a slanting roof, covered with tiles of shiny pearl shells and the four corners were curving up, each ornamented with a figurine at the tip. It was too far for Gavin to see the figurines clearly. He just felt strange but he couldn't tell what it was quite yet.

The white castle had been sketched with great care by Zoe. Long helped to beautify it because he knew Zoe wanted it for a royal family. He added some fine cravings under the roof and he extended the corners of the roof to make them curve up like those of ancient Chinese imperial buildings. Zoe didn't know much about ancient Chinese architecture but she could feel its magnificence. She had no idea that the roofs of Chinese palaces were golden yellow, a colour which Long suggested. That was why she'd insisted to keep it white. Zoe and Long worked with unspoken understanding as if they'd been doing this kind of thing for years. While Zoe was reading her next line, 'It was quiet and peaceful in front of Gavin but behind him, a swirl of black . . .' Long had already got the black pencil in hand, ready for the next illustration.

It had been quiet and peaceful for the whole morning but right now Gavin could feel his stomach suddenly in knots. Was it the intuition of an experienced story writer to foresee the storm after the calm? There was absolute silence but a dark swirl—a kind of tornado—was quickly creeping up on them from behind. A moment ago Gavin's attention was still entirely caught by the castle. Neither he nor the dragon had noticed anything approaching. But now, without thinking, Gavin turned to look back and this brought him face to face with the looming black cloud. He had no idea what it was but its sudden appearance was enough to make him fall from the dragon's back. Luckily the dragon was quick to react and caught Gavin with his tail.

The dragon then sped up and twisted to change direction so to get away from the dark looming force behind them. Gavin almost fell again but the dragon was able to tilt his body towards Gavin's falling side to keep him in balance. Gavin was gripping tight to the dragon's scales with his eyes closed and muscles all tensed up. 'Don't worry! The black thing wasn't after us.'

But it wasn't the black matter that Gavin was scared of since he didn't even know what it was, nor did he have the spare mindspace to think about it. He just couldn't stand the flying anymore. Gavin had never been confident about anything that involved balance skills. Up until now when his mind hadn't been on the job, his body was swinging automatically to keep himself balanced. Now, he had to think what to do, he couldn't manage it. 'Let's find a place to land,' he shouted.

The dragon glided over rows and rows of orchard trees, looking for a place to land. When Gavin opened an eye to have a peep, they were just above the lake. He could see from the reflection in the water's surface that someone else was flying, just above them. Before Gavin could see clearly, the object over them sped up and overtook them. Following it was that black cloud, now in the form of a long flowing ribbon. It was now flying ahead of the dragon. In fact this object—there was a person and he or she—was trying to show them the way to land. The black ribbon was tied to a . . . a broom? And riding on the broom, Gavin could see only the back of someone in black with a pointed hat.

"Gavin could see the back of someone in black with a pointed hat."

' . . . Gavin could see clearly now that flying ahead of them was a witch on a broom.' Long finished his sentence and passed the paper back to Zoe. He had all the time been thinking of an evil character to challenge Gavin.

'A witch . . . hm . . . I've a good idea. Let me draw her face.' Zoe had her coloured pencils ready.

The writer and illustrator were working more collaboratively now. As suggested by Zoe, the two had agreed to take turns writing lines of the story. It was just like what she and her classmates did during brainstorming sessions in class. So prior to meeting the witch, Zoe had created the black swirl but it was Long who made Gavin fall from the dragon. Zoe saved him though with a nimble dive of the dragon. Long was presenting Gavin's cowardice but Zoe knew the only problem for her father was balance. So far there were no conflicts and their story ran well.

Long was thankful to Zoe. Without her, he would never have actually started his writing. He thought a lot but he hesitated. She made him actually write. Zoe was enjoying the process. She had always wished to work with her dad like this. It was true he did listen to and adopt some of her ideas but not even once had he agreed to write together with her. To Gavin, Zoe was always a little girl.

Zoe enjoyed drawing with Long. For her, he was a great master with quick and skilful . . . not just skilful . . . but magical fingers. For the first time she could visualize her own pictures as if living out of the paper. Long didn't change anything she drew but just a few strokes in the background gave the perspective, made it rich with detail. Zoe was so pleased with their pictures that she kept posting them up on the wall, creating a big comic storyboard. Now as she passed her picture of the witch to Long, she could imagine her created character conversing with Gavin.

Gavin couldn't tell if he was feeling fear or joy. *Was she the witch they were looking for?*

'Come follow me!' The 'witch' turned and called out to the dragon.

To Gavin's surprise, she was just a young girl and too good looking to be a witch. The big smile made the witch look familiar to Gavin. But he couldn't tell right now where and when he had met her before. He was too busy to think. The black ribbon was flying towards him. But when the witch whistled, the ribbon just moved around Gavin and returned to her. As the shape swept across his face, Gavin could see clearly what it was—a large swarm of black butterflies. They landed on the witch's long gown and stayed still as if they were just a pattern on it.

Finally, they all landed in the orchard within the castle wall. The scent of fruits filled the air. Hanging on the different trees were apples, pears, peaches, apricots and fruits Gavin couldn't name.

'You are free to enjoy all our fruits here but the one I recommend is of course, the golden apple. You must try it.'

The girl led them to a tree in the centre. The apples on it were golden yellow. They smelt so sweet that the dragon could no longer resist the temptation to take a bite. Gavin was starving too. He was about to pick one but his hand halted in mid-air. He hesitated. *The girl might just be a young, good looking witch. Wait. How could he forget that? A witch could disguise and make herself look friendly and kind.* The girl had picked an apple for him. Now he noticed that she was wearing thick, black gloves on such a hot, sunny day, and he was sure the apples were poisonous. At once, he pulled the dragon away from the tree while staring suspiciously at the witch. She withdrew her hands and the friendly smile left her face. Gavin was backing away as he put his right hand on the hilt of his sword. He was about to draw ready to defend himself when he heard someone calling from behind.

'So you are back, Mariana?'

18

Who says that witches have to be wicked?

The young girl was overjoyed to hear her grandmother's voice. She ignored Gavin and ran past him to the old couple who were coming behind him. She gave them a big hug and they began talking as if they hadn't seen one another for a long time. While Gavin stood there looking at them, a guard came over to him, 'You dare not to kneel before the king and the queen?' Gavin was about to do so when he fell motionless to the floor.

'What? So the witch was a princess?'

'Yes. Is that a brilliant idea? We need to surprise the readers.'

It surprised Long at least. A moment ago, he was still preparing Gavin to fight the witch and her poisonous butterflies. 'So, was she a wicked witch?'

'Hmm . . . who says that witches have to be wicked?'

'So, the story will end—Gavin and the princess lived happily ever after in the white castle?' It would indeed be disappointing.

'No. Don't forget my daddy has to come back. But as a hero, he will have to help the princess in some ways first. There need to be some challenges.'

'You already know what the challenges are?' Writing with Zoe was itself a big challenge.

'Some.'

' . . . and how to tackle them?'

'No, not yet. But we'll think together . . . after dinner. I'm quite hungry now.'

'Good!' Long cried out in joy. So, that brief disappointment wasn't just because Gavin hadn't suffered enough but he hadn't created enough with Zoe.

Zoe was surprised by Long's reaction, 'You must be hungrier than me. Let's have a big dinner!'

'No, I'm not hungry. We can write more before we eat.' Long was keen to continue. 'Why was the witch a princess?'

But Zoe had already left the table and was looking into the fridge. 'There's a lot of stuff in the freezer. We can have hot pot. There're fish balls, crab sticks, cheese sausages, beef, pork, and wow, shrimps . . . . Hey, we still have two eggs. I like to dip the cooked meat in raw egg.'

'What about Gavin . . . ?' Long's mind was still in the story.

'He doesn't let me eat raw eggs. He says we may get Bird's flu.'

'Bird's flu? What's that? I'm asking why the witch was a princess and what had happened to Gavin?.'

'The story? . . . Can we prepare the broth first? . . . But Bird's flu is a good idea. We can keep writing while we are eating.'

Gavin felt himself stepping out into emptiness. He was falling but before he could hear his own screaming, he was already down in the water. He sunk and sunk until a big

bubble pushed him back up to the surface. He could feel the heat. The water was boiling. He struggled to swim against the swirl but he couldn't see where he was heading. All around him was a thick fog. Then a stream of wind dispersed the fog for a while and within that instant, he could see Zoe's smiling face looming forward. He sprang up from the water, hot and wet.

In front of him, it wasn't Zoe, but someone with a similar big smile. It was the witch. At once, she moved away. He had just been dreaming. Gavin could see the canopy of the four poster bed above him now. The dragon was by his bedside though most of its body was out in the balcony. Seeing the knight waking up, it moved its head closer, 'You have scared us. You fainted and you've got a fever.' Gavin touched his forehead. It was hot. No wonder he was all wet in a sweat.

When he turned back to the other side, the young witch had returned but the smile had gone. She had a crystal goblet in her hand, from which he could smell the sweetness of juice.

'It's the golden apple that I asked you to try. But you refused and that's why you became sick. Our kingdom has been under the curse of a deadly sickness. Now you can choose to trust me or you can choose to die.'

Gavin turned to look at the dragon. He had eaten the apple and he seemed fine. Gavin looked at the witch. If she wanted to harm him, she could have done it after he had passed out. So he might have accused a sincere person. The witch was still wearing her gloves. That might just be part of her clothing. He looked at her face. It was so unfriendly at the moment. But when he recalled that big smile he saw when he first opened his eyes, it reminded him of Zoe. That made him feel he could trust her. He started with a small sip. It was sweet and he was so thirsty that he soon emptied the crystal goblet in one big gulp.'

Zoe and Long were enjoying their hot pot, and of course, their story brainstorming. Zoe took a sip of her apple juice and continued, 'Gavin drank the apple juice. He knew the princess had saved his life. He said thank you but the princess still looked icy.'

As Zoe stopped, Long went on, 'Should we let the king and the queen come in now to introduce themselves and the princess?'

'Yes, good timing. I was thinking of something like that.'

'Does the princess have a name?'

'I haven't thought of one yet. We can just call her the princess in the meantime. Can you put the shrimps in?'

Holding back the witch who was intending to leave, the queen introduced her to their guest, 'This is our granddaughter Mariana. My dead son named her after me.'

'Mariana? Princess Mariana?' Gavin was puzzled. Even though Gavin had never met Princess Mariana, he had in mind how she looked. The witch in front of his eyes couldn't be his Mariana.

Misunderstanding Gavin's puzzled look, the king added, 'Are you wondering why she dressed like a witch?'

'I'm not dressed like a witch. I am a witch.'

Gavin could tell from her voice that she was still angry. He remembered that he still owed her an apology. 'I'm sorry

I'd doubted your good intention. Would you please forgive me, little princess?' That was the line he would use when he had to apologize to Zoe. It was effective to soothe Zoe every time and it worked on the princess too.

'Since you've apologized, I forgive you.' A big smile appeared on her face again. Gavin missed that smile so much.

Zoe was laughing heartily as she watched Long picking up and dropping the hot shrimp when he tried to remove its shell. 'Be patient. You should let it cool down a bit first.'

'It tastes better when it's still hot.' He removed the shell and gave it to Zoe.

'You're like my dad. If both of you were here now, then I'd have two hot shrimps.'

When your dad's back, I'll be leaving. Long felt a sudden feeling of loneliness.

Zoe put some watercress in Long's bowl. It had been a long time since someone put vegetables in his bowl. It hadn't happened even once since his mother's death. He chewed the watercress gently to let the sweetness last, it was like the taste of family.

'You're eating in such a funny way, like having a toothache. If my dad was here and you ate so slowly, he'd finish all the watercress before you got another bite. That's his favourite . . .'

Once she'd started, Zoe just kept talking happily about her dad's eating habits. Long was looking at her happy face behind the steam.

If your dad was here, you wouldn't see me. If your dad couldn't come back, would you have me in your family? Hey, am I wishing him not to return?

Zoe waved her hands in front of Long's face when she found him suddenly caught up in his thoughts. 'What are you thinking?'

'Nothing!'

'I know. You keep thinking why my daddy was sick and why the princess was a witch, right? Don't worry! I've the whole background story for that. It's long so I'll tell you and you can write it down.'

'Okay!' Long was happy to return to the story. It could distract him from the unwanted train of thought. And the story was something he and Zoe shared.

So Zoe began.

'The dragon asked the princess how she became a witch. The queen told them the story. "A few years ago, one of our peasants stole a golden goose from an ogre. The goose could lay golden eggs. But away from its master, it soon got sick. Not long after that, the goose died but the mysterious sickness was spread to other poultry. It spread over the whole village. The ducks died. The chicken died. Then the cows got sick and the pigs got sick. Soon the animals died and more and more people got sick. No doctors could cure the illness and people began dying."

There was only one person who could help . . .'

19

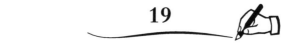

I know you must be here for a purpose

'. . . I remembered there was one person who could help. I went to the Green Fingered Witch and begged her for some curing herbs. I knew she only traded her herbs for something valuable to the person who asked for help. Many, many years ago, I gave her my memory for my lover's heart.' Queen Mariana took a glance at the king as she recalled her two meetings with the Witch.

Gavin followed her glance. It was Egbert, the descendant of the heartless dragon. Gavin looked at the queen. She was his courageous Mariana, only much older than he had pictured in mind. So his story had happened at least forty years ago. He was in doubt now that he had actually created them. They might have existed even without his interference, perhaps going through the same incidents, perhaps not. They had a life of their own, beyond his plot.

'. . . I thought I would never have to beg her again but I really couldn't think of another choice. I was prepared to give her anything—my life and the king's, anything except what she asked for. The witch wanted the heir to exchange for the herbs. Both Mariana's parents had died years ago. She was the only heir.'

' . . . The princess knew that the queen went to beg the green fingered witch and she wanted her to swap. So she went to the witch by herself.'

Zoe wasn't just telling the story but she started acting. She was now picking up a chopstick and holding it with both hands towards herself. 'She held a dagger in front of her chest. She was prepared to give the witch her life once she agreed to cure the people . . .'

Long found it very amusing. He could see that Zoe made a very brave princess. Now he believed that she would really have a long story to tell. She had actually begun to tell it in first person.

' . . . But the dagger turned into a slimy slug that slipped out of my hand. The witch emphasized that she wanted my life and not my death. She said I might live to be five hundred years old. Since I was prepared to give whatever she asked for, I made the blood vow with her.'

Zoe asked Long for his pen and drew a star on her left palm, a star she used to draw, with interlocking lines in one continuous stroke. Later she also drew it in Long's illustration. As usual, she didn't bother to make the ending point meet exactly at the starting point. There was a little gap.

' . . . I made the blood vow to be hers.' As Mariana continued, she removed her left glove and showed Gavin and the dragon a scar on her palm.

Gavin could figure it out that it had been a wound through which her blood mixed with that of the witch.

'Then she let me pick from amongst all her herbs the one that I wanted. I went through the whole garden, examining, sniffing and talking to the plants. Somehow I knew none of them made the proper choice. Then I could smell something sweet in the air and I could hear the whisper in the wind. I insisted I'd only take the apples from the tree in the southwest corner.'

'She must be very angry that you made the right choice.' The dragon interrupted.

'No, she's very happy to find the successor she was looking for.'

'That's how the princess became a witch. She put on the black gown and the pointed hat but then she couldn't take them off anymore.'

'It stuck to the skin?' Long was puzzled.

'No, but that's black magic. It's a story!'

Yes, I've got a magic feather also. Why am I having doubts? 'Sorry, I've asked a stupid question, go on.'

'The witch was nice to me, I mean, to the princess. She was free to visit the king and the queen from time to time. But she kept her promise and spent a lot of time with the witch, learning how to fly the broom, to cast simple spells and make different type of potions . . .'

'But the sickness still persisted?'

'Yes, because it was a curse from the goose. The people tried to plant more golden apples but the trees didn't bear any fruit. It was only after the princess had whispered to the trees that the fruit began to grow. That's why all the people love the princess even though she was a witch.'

'So it wasn't too bad to be a witch.'

'So it wasn't too bad to have a good witch in the kingdom.' The dragon commented.

But Gavin noticed that the old couple was wearing a worried expression.

Young Mariana's optimistic tone was fading also. 'I also thought that being a witch wasn't that bad. I could be a witch that cured, rather than killing. But finally I found out that I wouldn't stay good forever. Even now, my body, my mind and my heart are decaying and my evil side has begun to emerge.'

She removed the other glove to reveal her wrinkled, warty right hand with bony greenish fingers and long black nails. She held it to Gavin's face to scare him. 'It started from the little finger a year ago. From the witch's look, I know how it'll end. One day, everyone will be afraid of me.'

The fingers were scary but as Gavin knew her story now, he wasn't frightened at all. He held her hand in his. 'It doesn't matter how you look. You still have a beautiful heart.'

'No. One day my heart will become dark and I'll do all evil things.'

The king and queen tried to re-assure her, 'No, you won't.'

'But I've already done evil things.'

'Eating up a person? . . . Throwing someone in an oven? . . . Putting someone to sleep forever? . . . Turning someone into a frog? . . .' Long kept suggesting.

Zoe kept shaking her heads. 'It needed to be something less evil at the beginning.'

'Stealing? Lying?'

'They need no magical force. We can lie also.'

Yes I'm lying . . . but what else can I do?

'I know . . .' Zoe thought of something suddenly. 'It's just like we wish for something bad to happen and it happens.'

'We . . . made something bad to . . . happen?' Long paraphrased her line. He felt a sudden thrill.

'No, I mean the princess. She's a witch so she wished for something bad, she said it then it could be a spell. Now let's think of some bad wishes that hurt others . . .'

Long was still dwelling on her previous sentence. *We wish for something bad to happen and it happens.*

' . . . something like wishing a dragonfly to miss one wing so it can't balance . . . or . . . the hind legs of the cheetah to turn backwards . . . that's funny . . . then it'll be a tug of war between the front legs and hind legs . . . ha, ha, ha . . . Hey, what about a bird that sings with croak, croak, croak . . . ha, ha. Luckily, I'm not a witch.'

While Zoe was amusing herself with all these mischievous ideas, Long was caught in his own thoughts. *Getting Gavin hurt, making him suffer, wishing him to live happily forever in the story? What am I trying to write? What if that happened?* Long wished he had never started with the idea of writing the story.

Young Mariana lowered her head in shame as she recalled. 'The first time I cast a spell on an innocent canary and it got the voice of a toad. It was only a full day later I began to feel regret for my deed. But then I found out that I was not powerful enough to undo my spell. I promised myself I would never do it again but I couldn't control my own will. The second time, I turned a lovely rabbit to stone. No, even worse. I turned only its rear and hind legs into stone and watched its front half struggle to drag its stonified body along. I felt no sympathy but just kept laughing. This time it took three days before I realized how bad I was. Again I couldn't undo the spell.

The queen embraced her, 'That's why you stayed away from us for the last few months?'

'I'm afraid the next time, I may hurt a person and by then I may not even be capable of feeling sorry for causing others' sufferings.'

'We were so worried when you just disappeared.' The king joined in the embrace.

'I know. I miss you, too. That's why I came back . . . to say goodbye.' She couldn't bear to speak the last three words. She just whispered them to herself. Egbert and Mariana were still embracing her so they couldn't see her lips but Gavin saw it.

'Don't go to the witch anymore. Stop learning those spells. Stay in the castle and we can protect you.' The king commanded.

'It's no use. I've got the witch's blood in me.'

'A blood vow is still just a kind of black magic. Any magic can be done, it can be undone. For each spell there should be at least one way that it can be broken.' The dragon knew about the black magic because he had attended a wizard before.

'But the one who cast the spell could make or add conditions somehow impossible to be fulfill and then perhaps the spell couldn't be broken.' Mariana was a witch so she knew what she was talking about.

'Nothing is impossible in a fairy world'

'So you really think Gavin can beat the witch?'

'Of course, we shouldn't make it too easy for him. Otherwise he won't be heroic enough. But finally he will save the princess.'

'But what if it's all real?' Long wasn't too comfortable thinking about the possible risk. 'I mean . . . he's just your daddy. He's not a knight . . . He may . . .'

'Okay, okay . . . he's not too capable of fighting but he can outwit the witch. We'll think about that later. Now let me finish the last few sentences of this chapter.'

'However impossible it seemed, there would still be a chance. I was under a spell before. But this knight, who appeared so weak, was able to retrieve a sword from a rock and free me? He had undone two spells, the sword's and mine.' The dragon looked at Gavin, his adorable and brave knight, to seek his commitment to help the princess.

All eyes were on Gavin. Judging from his strange clothes, this knight must have come from a place far, far away.

'I know you must be here for a purpose.' Queen Mariana was confident.

'Yes, I'm here for the witch. I'll go to her and find the way to break the spell.' Gavin was surprised at the courage he'd found. He felt himself braver than he thought he was.

20

You're a liar

Long was relaxed when Zoe finally agreed to put away her writing pad and go for a bath. Before, he was the one eager to write the story. He started it just as a story. Then he was fascinated by the possibility of controlling the life of someone who had previously controlled his. He had wished to create all types of challenges and dangers for Gavin in the story. But Gavin deserved nothing more than just a bit of fright and flight, no real hazard. A premonition gradually built up in Long's mind when Zoe came up with all those dangerous ideas.

'. . . sneaking into a pit with thousands of poisonous snakes . . . going over a tight rope suspension bridge from one cliff to the other . . . just one careless step . . .'

What if Gavin really experienced those dangers? But Zoe was too enthusiastic to be stopped now. For her, it was just a story and whatever dangers, her daddy would be able to overcome them. *It would be difficult to convince her that a story character may really experience and act as written. Worse still, even an author may lose control.* There was only one thing Long could do. *It was time to tell her the truth.*

Gavin was alone in the room since the dragon preferred to stay outdoors, in the orchard. Moths and tiny insects were dancing around the flickering bedside lamp. Gavin used to hate that but now his mind was too occupied to feel bothered by them. *Where did I get that courage from? How can I manage the witch? But anyway I've come all this distance to look for the witch. Perhaps Periwinkle will have a way. But where's Periwinkle?*

Then he spotted the twinkling fairy flying in from the balcony among the insects. She came down gracefully as Gavin held out his palm for her. She was still spinning and dancing daintily on his hand. 'I'm so happy to see Mariana again after all these years.'

'That was forty years ago?'

'Time is meaningless to us.'

'I hadn't expected you'd look the same.'

'I'm a fairy. I'm immortal.'

'Have you spoken to her?'

'No, I've never thought of it. The moment she got back to the human world and retrieved her previous memory, she had to leave Fairyland behind, including any trace of memory about it.'

Gavin nodded in agreement. 'Anyway we've found the witch and I'm going to see her tomorrow.'

'I know. That's very brave of you to volunteer to help the princess. Have you thought carefully?' Periwinkle made him think again.

'I just felt . . . By the way, just now you were here?'

'Yes, all the time, among the flowers on the balcony.'

'No one saw you?'

'The mortals can't see us unless we want to show ourselves. But I didn't hide my presence from you. You must be too focused on other things. That's why you didn't notice me.'

'But I didn't even remember to look for you earlier. I'd totally forgotten about you.' Gavin confessed.

'Sometimes such things happen.'

'It wasn't for just one or two minutes. And it was not the first time.' Gavin recalled the time he lost Periwinkle in the dark tunnel and met the dragon on his own. Gavin had no doubt that things happening to him were beyond his control. But for the first time, he had a strange feeling that he might not even be in complete control of his own thoughts or actions.

'I know what you are thinking. I've had this feeling before. Like that time I was inspired to fly a different course. If not for that, I would not have happened to find Mariana at the forget-me-not field. That was not where I was intending to go. I believe that sometimes unexplained forces make us think or act or encounter something unexpectedly.'

'But that was not unexplained. I wrote you there.'

'Yes, that's what I told my friends—that I suspected external hands were acting on us. But none of them felt it that way. It may not happen all the time. Maybe not everyone has such experience. Or maybe not everyone is sensitive enough to notice.'

'Are you implying that we were acted upon by some external forces, forces that even control our minds?' Gavin asked tentatively to confirm his speculation.

'You should know it better than me because you have been the force itself. After all, you write across my path.'

'But do you mean, someone is now writing our story?'
'No, not our . . . I don't think I'm in this story. That's why you forgot my presence.'

'How come daddy has forgotten about me? One whole day and he hadn't called once.' The first thing Zoe did after the bath was to get into the study and check if she had missed any phone calls. She dashed by Long who was in the open kitchen wiping the plates and rehearsing his confession. 'My name's Long. I came out from . . .'

Before Long could respond or confess, Zoe was already in the study, disappointed by the 'zero' on the answering machine. *Daddy is too busy to make a call.* It had been that way ages ago but it was the first time since her mum's death. She sat on her dad's chair, trying to call him. She looked at the big story board on the wall. She couldn't wait to tell Gavin all about it. He would be proud of her. Again no one answered. When she was about to put down the phone, she heard a weak banging noise. What was that? She hung up the phone and it stopped. She called again. This time she held the phone away from her ear so that the ringing tone couldn't distract her. She could hear the soft banging again. She looked around and traced it to the fridge behind the chair. There it was, she saw her dad's mobile phone vibrating near the soda cans as she opened the fridge door.

Zoe knew immediately that it couldn't be a careless deed. *My dad isn't in Shanghai. He is missing. Has someone kidnapped him? KK said he had called from Shanghai so KK was lying. My friend had lied to me. Wait. My friend? I have known this mysterious man for just a day. I have befriended a bad guy whose partners might have kidnapped my dad.* But the happy moments they spent together were so genuine. She looked at the phone. She looked at the story pictures. Tears started rolling down her cheeks, tears for missing her dad and tears for her short friendship with Long.

Long put away the last plate, still murmuring his lines and struggling whether to say it now or wait for one more night. It was so quiet in the study. *Zoe might have fallen asleep. If so, then just ignore it for the moment? Perhaps Gavin would have found the feather and be back by tomorrow. It might be difficult for Zoe to accept the truth now.* Just when he turned around to leave the kitchen, Zoe was right in front of him, holding up her dad's phone, screaming at the top of her voice. 'You're a liar!'

Long stepped back, frightened by this sudden confrontation.

'Why are you so scared? Who are you? What have you done to my dad?' Zoe looked up right into Long's eyes. She had wiped her tears and was now acting firm and strong.

Long squatted down so his eyes were on the same level as Zoe's and took a deep breath. 'You have to believe in me. Your dad's inside the story world and I came out from one of his stories.' He bowed and his hands were held together in a traditional Chinese gesture for apology.

What this man said was ridiculous but Zoe knew it was true, at least the second part. His long hair, his strange gestures and way of talking, his ignorance of the modern city and common habits, how could she have missed the clues? He came from Nanjing, lived in the bamboo jungle with his friends and he could draw incredibly well and fast. Zoe was sure. 'You are Long, the talented artist?'

'It's Long!' Gavin murmured as he could only think of one person who could write about him. Of course, that was on the assumption that the author was someone he knew. He was the only person who knew he was stuck in the imaginary world. Now he'd had the idea, he sought the details that would confirm it. Gavin could see traces of design and patterns in his surroundings bearing ancient Chinese features that shouldn't have appeared in a Medieval Castle. There were embroideries of chrysanthemum patterns on the canopy and he recalled those curved up corners of the castle roof.

'Why is he writing your story?' Periwinkle asked.

'I don't know. Perhaps to express his anger. You find your life being controlled by someone and it's someone who made it tragic. If one day you had the power to control his destiny, what would you do?'

'I'm not sure I'd want to use that power. But if you've given him a bitter life, why should he write you as a hero?'

'Hmm . . . so he can kill me at the hands of the witch?'

'He could have killed you with the dragon's evil head. He could have made you lame or blind or scared you to death as a coward.'

Actually, Gavin knew it was true. Long might still be angry with him yet he had a good heart. But Long would never consider him a hero.

'Zoe, it's Zoe!' Gavin cried out in joy. 'That smile, the star on the palm, half rabbit half stone, . . . oh, yes, only Zoe had that imagination. Long would never have thought of them . . . . the blood vow, the green fingers, . . . she's a potential writer.' Gavin was proud of his daughter as he recalled all those details. 'She's got my genes.'

'I hope she won't make the same mistake.' Periwinkle made a comment which Gavin missed.

Long told Zoe everything since he stepped across the doorway and revealed that he had drawn such a doorway for Gavin to Fairyland. To Long's surprise, Zoe believed every detail he told her. Any sensible adult would probably explain the incident as an illegal immigrant breaking into the house. Unexpectedly, the owner was working at home so he was caught red handed. The owner was killed or kidnapped so there had to be other partners in the crime. The villain then stayed to make further ill gotten gains after he discovered that it was just a little girl who'd been left alone in the house. And now he was making use of the stories he had read on the computer to make up some nonsense to deceive the girl. If Zoe had called the police or any relative, Long would surely be put away for a long time.

But Zoe believed Long. She knew her dad and his stubbornness. She trusted Long and her feeling with him. She believed in the possibility of magical forces. Yet, she couldn't accept the fact that her dad would lose the feather if it was something so important. 'But how did you know?'

'I talked with him,' Long told her.

'You can talk with him?'

'I met him in Fairyland. Well, in my dream.'

'Oh! It's just a dream!' Zoe tried to soothe herself. 'It's true that he went to Fairyland but you just dreamt that he lost the feather.'

'But it's so real. And if not, why isn't he home yet?'

Zoe wasn't sure if she wished to believe in Long's dream. That proved at least her dad was in Fairyland and not just disappeared behind the magic doorway. But without the feather, how could her dad come back. 'I wish I could see him in *my* dream.'

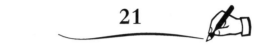

21

We can write to make the change

A black swirl flew in from the balcony and as the black butterflies settled themselves around the lamp, the room fell into darkness. Periwinkle remained twinkling around Gavin. Other than that, the moon was the only source of light. It cast a silver ring around the dim shadow of young Mariana, who was just flying in.

The room brightened up again as the butterflies returned to her side. 'I saw your light from outside so I knew you were still awake.'

'But you can still knock and come in that way.' Gavin pointed at the door.

'I know it's not so polite but I don't want to run into anybody in the hallway. It's a secret meeting.'

Gavin glanced at Periwinkle. She was still there so he assumed it was not a part of the story that had been written. Mariana followed his glance. 'It's just a firefly.'

'Oh, yes. So have you got something to tell me?'

'I came here to ask for your help.'

'You've got my promise. I will set you free from the witch.'

'How? How can you fight against her power?'

Gavin had been worrying about that also. But after surmising that the scenario was Zoe's creation, he had become less worried. He just had to confirm it. 'Can you show me your scar on your palm one more time?'

The princess showed him. The gap between the starting and ending points, the proportion of the overlapping lines and the orientation of the vertices, it was definitely drawn by Zoe.

'I'll do whatever the witch asks and give whatever the witch wants in exchange for your freedom.' Gavin was confident. He knew Zoe would give her hero a hard time. He was prepared to face some creepy creatures and go through some risky adventures but he was sure his little writer would leave him in one piece. There might be some twists along the way but the final victory would be his.

Gavin peeked at Periwinkle to seek her support but she was shaking her head.

Mariana made a fist to hide her scar. 'You don't have to do that for me. It's not brave. It's mindless. The witch may leave you alive but with all your limbs dissolved or she could keep you as the eyeball bearer to provide re-growing eyeballs, to feed her crow ever day. If that's not enough to scare you off, read more.' She threw him a book with the cover made of chameleon skin. It fell on the bed and took up the same colour and pattern as the bed sheet. 'And she would never consider your sacrifice worth to exchange for my freedom.'

Gavin saw Periwinkle nodding in agreement.

'Then what kind of help do you want from me?'

'Keep this book and hide it in a place I won't be able to retrieve it.'

Gavin opened it and had a quick look. Catatonic spells, nightmare spells, transfigurations, hypnosis, petrification, dreamobilizing, mud gobbler, . . .

'After I realized that whatever I did to slow down the process I would still lose my mind and heart totally one day, I learnt the black magic and potions. I've worked hard at my lessons these last few months. And of course I learnt the ways to undo each spell. In this book I have written all I know about the undoing of spells. It isn't everything but I can't be sure now how much more time I have. Ten days ago, I enslaved a passer-by with some heart burning potion. The potion caused unbearable pain when he refused to take my orders or tried to escape. He was released and given the antidote when I came to my senses two days ago. Next time, the evil in me might gain control permanently. That's why I came back to say goodbye to my grandparents.'

'So I'm lucky to meet you today and not a few days ago . . . .'

' . . . or some days later.'

'You wanted to keep that book somewhere so at least people have a chance to learn to undo some of the black magic.'

'Not everyone can learn such tricks and ingredients for some antidotes are difficult to collect. But those desperately in need will find the hope and a chance through what I have written. At first I planned to leave it to my grandparents but since you've come, a person brave and kind to offer help, I think you will make a better choice. I can keep the secret from them longer. Besides, in the future if I remember there is such a book, I may try to retrieve and destroy it. I may hurt my grandparents if they are the custodians.'

'So you plan to go back to the witch?'

'Yes, except for those who came to us for a purpose, good or evil, the others should be safe. I'll continue to write down my newly learnt magic and hide what I've written away when my mind allows. But in case I don't have further chances or in case I destroy the future copies, there's this one that you will have hidden or passed on. Remember, I may live up to five hundred years.'

Gavin was wondering how her story would proceed but he was deeply impressed by her idea of writing to change the future. 'Don't worry! I'll hide it for you. By the time I'm leaving this world, I'll make sure it's in good hands.

'I'd appreciate that. Now ask me for something in return for your favour.'

'You've saved my life.'

'The apple juice? That didn't count. Everyone here can save you with that.'

'I'm not doing it to gain anything.'

'But you must. That's a trade. If you don't keep your promise, you'll be cursed.'

'Ask her for some dreamosemary.' Periwinkle was whispering at Gavin's ear to remind him.

'Then can I have some dreamosemary?'

'That's a good choice. You won't be able to get it anywhere else.' After saying this, Mariana went to fetch the pillow from Gavin's bed and torn it opened. From amongst the feathers filling it, she took out a dry crescent shaped leaf. It was around the length of her little finger and dark purple in colour. 'Did you dream of anyone or any place?'

Gavin recalled the smiling face of Zoe from behind the fog.

Mariana was waving the leaf in front of her nose. 'Sweet dream for the homesick traveller. It might lose its effect after such a long time. Don't worry! I'm going to pick you a fresh one from the witch's garden tomorrow. Don't go over to her cliff. Wait for me above the waterfall. In the meantime, sleep tight.'

'We can't just sit waiting. We must do something.' Zoe said and she did. She knew that neither police nor friends could help because they wouldn't be searching in the right place. She was determined to save her daddy by herself, or at least with Long's help. She took down some of the pictures and asked Long to draw on the same wall, though this time with a normal paintbrush. They could see the doorway into Fairyland on the other side. But of course, they couldn't get through.

Zoe was lying on the couch. She fixed her eyes on the Fairyland picture for a while and closed her eyes. Long was lying on the floor, reading the Fairyland book for the third time. They tried to sleep to get there. But not only couldn't they dream of it, they couldn't sleep at all in their agitated state of mind.

Zoe kept opening her eyes to look at the pictures.

'We need to relax and be more patient.' Long suggested. But he knew that if he had been more patient and forgiving, he would have stayed and helped Gavin find the feather. He wished for another dream to make up for the chance he lost last time.

Zoe opened her eyes again. This time she sprang up excitedly with a sudden inspiration. 'We can write to make the change.'

Zoe got to the computer and continued on her daddy's work. She read as she typed, ' . . . Long came out to Gavin's study. He lent the feather to Gavin . . . Zoe was very worried after she knew her daddy couldn't come back. She prayed to God for some magical power. After that, Zoe could feel the power in the paintbrush she was holding. She asked Long to draw again. A magic doorway appeared and they stepped through it into Fairyland.'

Once she finished the writing she held the paintbrush and convinced herself it had the power her writing had given it. She asked Long to try the drawing again but of course, it didn't work.

Zoe wasn't ready to give up. She tried a few more times, adding more details to the story, convincing Long to think and act more sincerely.

Gavin couldn't believe it. He almost cried out in joy. That was the doorway in front of him. He could see his study behind it. Long was crouching there. He was drawing from the other side. Zoe, eyes closed, was about to step across. Gavin ran forward, ready to hug his little girl as she came through the door. Now he was in the room but Zoe was not in his arms.

'Ouch!' Zoe cried.

Gavin turned and saw Zoe bumping onto the wall. 'Zoe, . . .' He called but he couldn't hear his own voice. He only heard Long's.

'Should we stop? We've tried many times.' Long was rubbing Zoe's forehead gently.

Gavin realized that the foreheads of both Zoe and Long were swollen and red from bumping into the wall where they thought the doorway should be.

'But daddy also wrote to make things happen.'

'Yes but I shouldn't have . . .' Gavin tried to respond.

Zoe and Long didn't seem to hear him. Gavin couldn't hear himself. He saw Zoe coming towards him, walking through him and back to the computer.

Gavin was left standing there disappointed. He raised his hands in front of his eyes. He saw nothing but the door and the view of Fairyland. They were vanishing and an empty wall was left. No, it wasn't totally empty. There were a few newly added pictures on one side. The face of a young witch, a big close up of the dragon . . .

Gavin opened his eyes. The dragon was blocking most of the sun and the view. But he could tell it was morning and he was still lying on the bed in the castle. It had all been just a dream.

22

Come over, if you want anything from me

'My daddy's not in Fairyland now.' Zoe was sure. 'He's in the White Castle. Remember, we wrote him there and he's going to help the princess. That's why he forgot about the feather and about coming home.'

Long had had that impression also. That's why he wanted to stop Zoe from writing that part of the story. But at the same time he found it hard to convince himself of the possibility of their intervention. He had wished for it but he was also scared to accept owning that power of having caused things to happen. 'So now we have stopped writing the story, he should be coming back soon.'

Without thinking, they both turned and looked at the wall. No one was coming through.

'We might need to help him a bit.' Despite the poor prospects of success, Zoe would rather try than wait. She got back the writing pad and continued, 'The princess reminded Gavin of his dear daughter. Gavin remembered he didn't belong to the story world. He took out the feather, got some water and drew the doorway home.'

They looked at the wall again. Nothing happened.

'Hey, he still hasn't found the feather.' Long was still sure what he had known from the dream was real. He took the writing pad from Zoe and added some more lines. Before Zoe's last sentence, he wrote. 'Thinking about the feather lost in Fairyland, Gavin soon fell asleep. He returned to Fairyland in his dream. The fairies were glad to see him and showed him the feather they had found . . .'

They waited but still there was no sign of Gavin.

'Maybe he wanted to save the princess first.' Of course, Zoe would like to imagine her daddy, a brave and unselfish saviour, delaying his return because he had a noble mission. She didn't want to think of him as a helpless wanderer, lacking the means to return.

Gavin was still recalling every detail of his dream. That dried dreamosemary leaf was still working. He had left it under the pillow. He got it out, kissed it gently and put it in his pocket, together with the feather. While getting the leaf, he could feel Mariana's book under the pillow also.

'Quick! We have to go to the witch!' The dragon was urging its hero.

Gavin looked around. He was looking for Periwinkle.

There on the balcony, she was flying out from a petunia that had just begun to bloom. 'Are we going to hide the book now?'

'What book?' The dragon asked.

Gavin moved the pillow to reveal it but of course, without knowing a book was there, the dragon couldn't see it.

Gavin told the dragon Mariana's plan.

'So you're not going to free the princess from the witch?' the dragon asked disappointedly.

Gavin knew that the dreamosemary in his pocket was still working. He didn't need to take any risk. They could head back to Fairyland and hide the book in the dragon's lair on their way. Periwinkle could take the herb to Long, who could then get to Fairyland and draw him the doorway. After that, he could still save Mariana. He would have that power in his world. He could write and create a real hero to save her through his story. He could even mock that coward knight who had fled without saying goodbye. He would be just an insignificant side character in 'The story of the Witch Princess'.

But Gavin remembered the story illustrations he saw in the dream. From that smile on the young witch's face, Gavin knew how Zoe had projected herself in this character. He believed she had written him as a brave hero, promised to finally free Mariana from the witch.

Gavin in the real world was not physically strong. He seldom exercised, was poor at sports, never even played fighting games on the computer. He was scared of snakes and spiders, wouldn't dare to stop someone near him in the cinema from talking on the phone. He lacked even the courage to talk about death. But Gavin, the knight, would beat the witch. He had survived the dragon's attack. He had pulled out a sword from a rock. So he should be able to save the princess whatever challenges lay ahead. After that happy ending, he could still go back to Fairyland and follow the original plan.

'You are here for a purpose. You have to save the princess.' The dragon always trusted his instinct.

'Are you sure you'll be able to defeat the witch?' Periwinkle wanted to keep Gavin focused on the task at hand.

'If I was written to . . .'

'But what if you weren't?'

He knew that his present struggles couldn't have been entirely written. That's why he was hesitating. He wished to know what he was supposed to do. If only he could know the plot . . . But Gavin knew that he had to work with whatever was written in order to be part of the solution.

'Forget about finding that feather. Perhaps it's been destroyed or lost forever. But if we're trying to help, we can just give my daddy another one.' Zoe believed that they had to be more proactive.

'Why should the Phoenix Goddess give Gavin a feather?' The question seemed reasonable to Long.

'It doesn't need to come from your phoenix. The king and queen should have a lot of treasures from all over the world. They may happen to have another phoenix feather.'

'A magical one?'

'Yes, there are magical things all around, magical beans, a lamp with a genie, a knife that can open ways to another place . . . Sometimes people just don't notice them or their hidden power. At first you didn't know the feather was magical.'

Long had to admit it. And he had to agree, 'We're trying to do magic too.'

They began to write other versions, creating scenarios for Gavin to meet a kind fairy, two friendly elves, a helpful unicorn . . . Zoe was trying to write everything she could think of. But still there was no sign of Gavin.

Gavin had decided to meet the princess at the waterfall first. He had the excuse that the fresh dreamosemary she was going to bring him should be more effective. Gavin was postponing his decision to see if he was written to take further action. As far as Periwinkle was concerned, Gavin had already made the choice.

'I've picked these for you.' Mariana handled a small bunch of fresh leaves to Gavin. 'This is the fresh dreamosemary. Smell it!' After putting it in Gavin's hands, she held his hands up towards his nose. Among the dark purple crescent shaped leaves were some attractive pink flowers with heart shaped petals.

'Zoe, I missed you so much.' All of a sudden, Mariana seemed shorter, smaller. Gavin was holding her up in the air. Under that pointed hat was Zoe's face.

The dragon was shocked to see Gavin's reaction. Periwinkle flew to his side. 'She's not Zoe. It's an illusion.'

A broad grin appeared on Zoe's face and then the next moment, her face turned green and wrinkled. The upper eyelids loosened and dropped until two narrow slits took the place of the big curious eyes. The nose dissolved into a horrid cavity. The grin remained but on a face with a toothless mouth with bad breath.

Gavin threw the witch hard on the ground. But Zoe's face was there again. She was on the ground where she'd been thrown and crying piteously.

'It's an illusion, let's go.' Both the dragon and Periwinkle were ready to turn and leave at once but Gavin just stood there, staring at this poor Zoe whom he knew but could not accept was not his daughter.

He saw the face alternating between that of a crying Zoe and a laughing ugly creature. He wanted to hug his daughter but he wanted to get away from this ghastly apparition. When he tried to run it was as if his legs were pinned on the ground. He gripped the herbs tightly in his left hand.

Periwinkle flew around the hand. Her wings were glowing brightly, the aura was distinguishable even in the bright daylight. A musical tinkle was heard. Gavin's fist loosened and the herbs dropped on the ground.

Periwinkle pulled Gavin by the sleeve and he ran, ready to mount on the dragon.

The witch below resumed Mariana's face. She was pleading in tears. 'You have seen how I will look like. You said you would save me from the witch.'

Gavin paused. He knew he should have gone but he had come to meet the princess one more time. That was his purpose for being here. 'Bring me to the witch. I'll try to negotiate with her.'

'That's not the help Mariana wanted from you.' Periwinkle reminded him. 'She's trying to trick you.'

'What did she want you to help with, then?' It was an echo from an overhanging cliff on the opposite side of the chasm. They looked up and saw a short, humpbacked silhouetted figure in a row of willows at the edge of the cliff. Gavin looked at Mariana. She was shaking her head gently. The black butterflies began revolving around her and soon formed into a tornado that took her back to the overhanging cliff.

'Come over, if you want anything from me! Or leave now if you lack the nerve!' The voice echoed between the two cliffs.

The dragon was ready to lift off. But the moment it extended its wings, a beam was reflected on it and it was turned to stone. It became a rock statue standing on one leg on the cliff above the waterfall.

'I can't come over to you without my friend's help.' Gavin called out to the witch.

'Whoever comes to me must take that bridge.'

Gavin recognized the bridge. It was actually just a rope suspended from this side of the ravine up to the witch's cliff. Nobody had ever minded it was too narrow to be functional at all because no one had ever had to get to the other side. Gavin had created it for his Mariana to demonstrate her courage and determination. He didn't actually describe how she got across, whether by walking or by hanging and climbing. He wished he had researched the possibility of using it in practice. Now it just seemed impossible for him.

But both Marianas had done it. He believed that Zoe would have empowered him with the courage and ability to do it. *She wants to see my courage and confidence. It's just a matter of belief. Just imagine I'm a brave knight. I've survived the dragon. I've pulled out the sword. It's a fairy tale. I can do it.* Gavin kept murmuring but he knew it was different this time. He tried to convince himself it was a written part but he knew it wasn't. He looked at Periwinkle to seek her agreement.

23

You need to learn treasuring what you have

'Hey, it can be more direct. My daddy might not need magical items to work out the magic. He may accidentally go through a door or a mirror, go in a wardrobe or fall into a hole, or walk across a bridge, etc. And whatever the method, they are all leading here.'

'That wall?'

'No, it'll be more reasonable to have corresponding ends. If he went into a wardrobe, he should come out from one of our wardrobes, from a mirror to a mirror, a door to a door, a bridge . . . can't think of it, leave this.'

Zoe and Long wrote and waited and checked one after another but none brought Gavin back.

'Maybe your daddy's the only one who has that power, the power that comes through writing. Our stories have no effects at all. You can imagine if two persons are writing opposite things about the same person, what's going to happen to him?' Long felt more comfortable with this doubt.

'Maybe you're right but in that case, what can we do? Wait? . . . Till when? Go to the police? Call my grandma? . . . And you don't have any ID? No adults will believe our story. They will think we are crazy and lock us in a mental hospital.'

Long didn't understand exactly what she was talking about but from Zoe's expression, he knew those magical ideas were also unbelievable to other people in this world. It was different from pressing a button to make people suddenly appear in or disappear from that black box called TV. 'There's really nothing else we can do?'

'This is a magical accident so it can only be solved through magical means.' Zoe insisted. She wished she knew some fairies, witches or wizards in real life. She knew there were such people living in the world. 'We can't just go to every person and ask them if they can do real magic or know anybody who can. They won't tell and some may even be evil magicians . . .' She kept murmuring for a short while until she came up with a new idea, ' . . . Hey, let's check the internet.'

'Internet?' Long had no idea what it was. He didn't know that this black box could be more than a story book. But now he was fascinated by the magic it could play when various pages of words and pictures appeared, flashing up each in quick succession. Was it some kind of fortune telling?

Some articles were too difficult for Zoe and those she could understand were not very useful. 'They lived centuries ago . . . this is fake . . . dress up party . . . Scotland, too far away . . . Germany, Europe again . . . Africa, they may not know Fairyland . . .'

Long was lost. He didn't understand anything Zoe was saying but could this kind of divination help?

After some time, Zoe cried out again. 'I know one person who will help!'

'Who?'

'J.K. Rowling. I know Harry Potter is not real. But Rowling should know some of these people from the research for her books. She may even know the magic herself. I'll write to her. I'm sure she'll help because she's an author like my daddy.'

'An author?' Long doubted. 'What can an author do?'

'I can try my best!' Periwinkle knew the best help she could give at present wouldn't be to persuade Gavin to leave but rather to help him with what he was still working out to do. Gavin was making his choices in spite of the danger ahead.

Periwinkle's wings were emitting a bright glow again. She sang and her high chime-like voice was soon echoed by different kinds of low humming, buzzing, chirping, hissing, etc. All types of flying insects swarmed from every direction to settle and hover near the rope. Gavin realized that they were helping to extend the width of the rope. Big and strong ones like some giant beetles, locusts and cockroaches crowded near the rope and supported on each other to form the scaffolding. Those with big wings but no strong exoskeleton like the butterflies and dragonflies hovered at the edge for balance. Smaller insects like the bees and wasps filled the gaps of the scaffolding while still tinier ones like the mosquitoes and flies filled in their gaps. It was like a floating block about thirty centimetres wide and thirty centimetres thick, extending out from their side of the rope, maybe for a length of a metre. Gavin could expect that as he moved forward, those insects at the back would fly to pave the way ahead. He should be better supported than a mere rope to go all the way to the other side.

'That's all I can do.' Periwinkle stopped the singing when the number of new arrivals began to diminish.

'Thank you.'

It was still extremely demanding for Gavin but not impossible. He couldn't turn back now that he had chosen to come. He thought of Zoe looking forward to him as a brave hero. If he could overcome this fear, he should have the courage for everything. He walked closer to the edge.

Periwinkle knew just courage was not enough. Gavin would need more confidence and focus to get there. 'By yourself, you may not be able to do it. But trust me, I'm a fairy. And see all these little friends. They're not here to see you fall but to support you. Trust them.'

*"Gavin was ready to rely on Periwinkle and
the insects beneath his feet."*

The first few steps were the most difficult. At first, Gavin doubted if the insects could support his weight, but they did. Though every step was like walking on a narrow string of mattress, with loosened springs, suspended over a fatal drop, it was less stretchy than he had expected. When Gavin looked down to watch his steps, the fall of over three hundred metres beneath his feet made him freeze. Then he tottered and he almost fell but the insects were quick to shift their positions until he regained balance. Periwinkle flew backwards in front of Gavin like a humming bird. 'Don't look down! Don't look to your sides! Just look at me and move on.' Gavin didn't watch his steps anymore. He was ready to rely on Periwinkle and the insects beneath his feet.

Gavin could never have believed that he could maintain balance but as his feet sank and wobbled with each moving step he knew he was managing it. Just a few more steps. The wind was getting stronger but everything should be fine. Then he felt the first few drops of rain on his face, and then it started pouring down. Periwinkle sped up and he followed. He ran the last few steps. When he stepped on the far cliff and looked back, all the insects had dispersed. They couldn't fly once their wings were wet. He had made the last two steps on the real rope, and all by himself.

'Thank you. Help me to say thank you to your friends.' Gavin was holding Periwinkle on one palm and sheltering her with the other hand.

'Not my friends, they're our friends.'

Gavin nodded in agreement. He was sure he wouldn't swat another bug ever and, if he ever got home, he would throw his pesticide away.

'It's raining hard. Come here and have a hot drink.' The witch was calling to them from far away but they could hear her well. Gavin had come so far, he was ready to go further.

Having run past rows of willows, Gavin and Periwinkle were now among trees of ascending height. Gavin knew that if he kept on going into the wood he would come to the witch's hut. If he could come out of the wood, he would still have a chance to go home. If he could not, then neither would Long. Gavin stopped and found a place well sheltered from the rain. He took out the feather and put Periwinkle on it. 'Help me to take the feather to Long.'

'You think he'll come to save you?'

'You and our friends have taught me about trust. Long had entrusted the feather to me in the first place but I had doubted him. And all the time I wouldn't trust him to send him the feather. The problem doesn't lie with him, it's my fault. I know he'll come to help me get home.' Gavin paused to picture what would happen. 'But don't bring him into the wood. By sunset, if you don't see me coming out, tell him to draw his way home directly.'

Gavin handed Periwinkle the dried dreamosemary and continued. 'Give this to Zoe so she may see her mummy and me in her future dreams. But don't let her come. It's most important. Don't let her come. Use your sleeping dust. If we're lucky, she'll see me by her bedside when she wakes up. If not, hopefully, she can hear my last words in her dream so she won't need to look for me.'

Gavin found a dry rock. The feather was still wet from the rain with water dripping. He drew a hole big enough for his thumb and the index finger to poke through and then he held the end of the feather. He pictured the corner of his study in his mind and pushed the feather, together with the leaf and Periwinkle, through the hole. 'Thank you very much, Periwinkle.'

'Don't worry, we'll meet . . . .' Before he heard all her words, Periwinkle, the feather and the leaf were all gone into the rock. The round water mark soon dried up.

Gavin went on and soon came to a fence of waist height, wound with all types of vines. A mixed scent saturated the moist air. It was sweet but at the same time putrid and acrid. The garden was big with plants covering every inch of ground, except the footpath. Gavin kept on the path even though it was paved with bones and skulls because he wouldn't want to touch any of the vegetation. Out of place in the big garden, at the end of the bone-paved path was a small, shabby hut, wrapped in thick layers of moss.

The door squeaked as it swung open before Gavin knocked on it. The room was dim even though it was daytime because the windows were covered with moss. The only source of light was a fire at the fireplace. Gavin went in and couldn't avoid stepping on the plants anymore because the floor was carpeted with fungus and grass. Just in front of the fireplace was a low table, which was actually the bottom part of the trunk of a big fallen tree. Sitting at the table, on the side of the fireplace, was the old humpbacked witch. She was in a ragged and mouldy black gown. Frizzy white hair was straggling out from under her shabby pointed hat. She raised her head, gave Gavin an intimidating look and gestured him to sit opposite to her. Gavin sat down on the protruding part of a tree root. He could see the witch's face better now. Her densely wrinkled face was ghoulish and green, covered with purple warts and red blisters. A crooked nose was the most distinguishable feature marking its centre amongst the heap of loosened skin. Above the nose, were two opaque eyes, half buried under heavy eyelids and below the nose was a lipless mouth with collapsed jaws and heavy jowls.

"Frizzy white hair was straggling out from under her shabby pointed hat."

Soaked by the rain and shivering in a place that was damp despite the fire, Gavin felt a chill down his spine. Wanting to get through his ordeal as quickly as possible, he came straight to the point. 'I've come here to beg for your mercy to let the princess go.'

'Have some hot soup. It keeps you warm.' The witch filled his bowl with some soup from the cauldron behind her before she went on. 'It was her own choice to agree giving me her life in exchange for all the lives in the kingdom.'

'But she's not willing to anymore.'

'It's just a transition. She will soon get used to her new identity. One day she will have completely forgotten that painful transition.' The Green-Finger Witch believed that she had forgotten hers. But had she? The witch had no name nor could she recall her past. She couldn't even remember having had a past or a name to forget until that day when she saw the princess putting on her witch gown. It was true that she still couldn't remember her name or her past. But she could no longer deny that she had had them before and she knew the princess was now on the same path. It might be painful but she would forget.

'I've come to bargain for her freedom?' Gavin went on even though the witch seemed distracted.

'What can you offer?' The witch was glad to go on with bargain.

Gavin looked around him. 'A big, warm castle with a huge garden, lots of maids, elegant clothes, jewellery, . . .'

'Ha, Ha, Ha . . . look, it's such a cosy place here. Just because you can't appreciate it doesn't mean I'm not happy with it. If I'd wanted what you're offering, I would have asked and got it in the first place.' Actually she had chosen to live away from those good things, things that might help her old memory sneak back. It had been a long time, so long that she couldn't even remember there'd been such things in her life.

'Then what do you want? You can have anything, as long as it's not someone's life or will or freedom, or memory or love or emotion or . . .'

'Quite a list of exceptions!'

'I need to be cautious.'

'You're very cautious! If you don't trust me, then why do you come to bargain with me?' She laughed mysteriously, took a sip of her soup. Then she took off her grin and commanded. 'Finish the soup!'

Gavin dared not touch a thing. He was not prepared to take the risk of eating anything from a witch's cauldron. He tried to refuse politely, 'No, thank you but . . .'

'Then you can leave!' The witch's voice was firm but she knew he wouldn't leave.

'I can write . . . no, I can give . . .'

'If you don't trust me, I can't trust you.' The witch pointed to the door.

Gavin knew he had no choice. Anyway if the witch wanted to kill him, she didn't need any poison. With just a simple spell, he would have become a stone or a toad already. Gavin closed his eyes and emptied the whole bowl in one big gulp. He wouldn't want to know if he had swallowed an eyeball or a spider. A slight tingle went down his throat and into the stomach. Then he really felt much warmer.

'Good! Now we can continue.' The witch resumed her grin. 'I've never broken any promises. I've always made fair deals which both sides agreed to freely. After I've given the people what they asked for, they regretted what they'd agreed and tried to break their promises.'

Gavin knew the witch was telling the truth but he didn't feel like saying anything yet as the tingle remained in his throat.

The witch continued. 'You cannot be too greedy. You must be ready to pay. If you get one thing of value, you should be ready to give away another of equal value.'

Somehow she knew it even though she didn't know how she had learnt it.

Was it the effect of the soup? Gavin felt he was agreeing with the witch. He was opening his mind to something he had never thought of before. He couldn't tell if it was still the witch talking or another voice speaking in his mind. 'One pays and he gets something, he thinks it's fair. One gets something first and when he has to pay, he just sees the loss.'

Gavin's vision became blurred but clear flashbacks came into his mind. The voice over continued. It was a vague sensation, as if there were some unseen narrator explaining what things meant. 'When one loses something, he asks why it is being taken away but he forgets to ask why it is given to him when he gets it . . .' Like turning over pages in an old album, Gavin saw his childhood, his parents and sister, examinations, graduation, career, marriage, the birth of Zoe, sickness and death of Sofia, reading with Zoe, walking across the doorway, then back to his present scenario of sitting in the witch's room.

Gavin also heard himself voicing a protest. 'But can we have a choice of what to pay, what to get, what to keep and what to lose?'

'What's the use to give you the choice if you will never make it right? You'll always find what you have got or kept of a lesser value than what you haven't got or what you have lost. You don't need to learn making the right choice. You need to learn treasuring what you have.'

Gavin found his vision was getting clearer again as he kept blinking to force away the tears. He regained his focus and saw the witch sitting opposite to him, waiting for him. The tingling had vanished. 'What was in the soup?'

'Some spices and hot pepper to keep you warm. But of course, if you found they are having side effects on your mind, I hope they are more beneficial than harmful.'

Gavin remembered what he was supposed to do, to convince the witch to strike a bargain. 'Why do you just have to wish for things that others treasure, things they'll be lost without? Why don't you wish for something you really want for yourself? Forget about the others!'

'There's only one thing I wish for and no one has it . . . Immortality!'

'When I return to my place, I can make you immortal . . .' Gavin fired back. He wasn't totally empty handed when he decided to come. As long as she was persuaded to let him go first, he was sure he could satisfy her.

'You can grant immortality? What kind of power do you think you're talking about? Who do you think you are?' The witch was pressing close to Gavin, staring him in the eyes. 'Are you ready to pay for having that power?'

Gavin kept moving back even though the witch wasn't coming nearer. In the beginning, it was a greedy thought. He wrote without knowing its effect but which did bring Long to his world. Then he abused the effect and got into this other world. He came to realize the power through writing and now he was thinking of exercising it. This time, he might excuse himself with a kind purpose. But what would follow? He was not backing away from the witch but from the temptations in his mind, the temptations to interfere with lives.

But anyway the witch showed no interest in Gavin's offer because it was not necessary. 'I don't care if you really have that power. But you do have one thing to exchange for the princess' freedom, the phoenix feather.'

24

Desire can distort your senses

The feather was lying in a corner of the room.

Periwinkle was flying around in the room, exploring a world she had never imagined. She could feel a cool breeze but the air wasn't fresh. She flew towards the light but saw no dancing flame. She could smell lavender but traced it to just some rattan sticks in a bottle of fragrance oil. So strange and unnatural! This wasn't a place she would like to stay.

At the coffee table, Long was busy drawing. This was the only thing he could think of doing. Picture after picture, he had drawn of Gavin finding and going through different types of passageways back to the real world. He was creating as many scenes as possible, hoping that one of them would actually happen. He reviewed all the illustrations of the story. He saw a familiar creature among the other Chinese mythical figures on the castle roof corners. He was now so wrapped in the effort of trying to make a phoenix come to life that he didn't notice Periwinkle landing on his pen. He just waved the pen to get rid of what he took to be a loathsome fly.

Zoe was still surfing for information about fairies and witchcraft. It was almost midnight and she was struggling against her sleepiness. She didn't want to lose any time but her eyelids were getting heavier and dropping. After a minute, her head dropped and that action wakened her. After she had struggled to open her eyes fully, she slapped her face and shook her head to wake herself up further. But the process soon repeated itself. Periwinkle was hovering in front of the computer screen, examining those enlarged figures which resembled her kind. Zoe's head dropped again. This time through the narrow slit of her opening eyes, she saw a flower fairy flying out from the screen. She was wide awake at once but still she slapped her face. She wanted to check if it was a dream.

'A flower fairy! . . .' Zoe cried out in joy.

Long turned in Zoe's direction.

Zoe had lowered her voice, with the fear that she might scare the fairy. 'A flower fairy had come to help!'

Long wasn't sure this was what he heard. Zoe was whispering and he hadn't seen Periwinkle yet because the computer monitor was blocking his view. When he got over to Zoe's side, he was also stunned by the sight of this tiny fairy, who was now sitting on Zoe's palm. 'Are you from Fairyland?' Long had seen similar fairies in his last dream. Periwinkle nodded with a smile.

'From Fairyland! I thought you had come out from the website. But, yes, how could I miss that? I have seen you in the illustration.' Zoe looked at the fairy from head to toe. 'You're Periwinkle!' Zoe was sure that she shouted out in joy.

Both Long and Zoe were optimistic now that Gavin would be back in the next minute. It was likely that Periwinkle was sent here first and could Gavin follow? Long felt relieved with the expectation that Gavin had never encountered the danger he and Zoe had created.

'Is my daddy on his way?'

'It is a long story.' Periwinkle led them to the corner. A sense of misgiving flooded in once they saw the feather there by itself.

'The Phoenix feather?' Gavin glanced at his pocket without thinking. He felt relaxed to remember that it wasn't there. 'What feather? I don't have any feather.'

'Don't belittle my ability and don't overestimate my patience. That's the only thing I want from you, nothing else.'

'No, I can't let you get across.' To Gavin that was the feather's only value.

'Get across to where, to where you come from? That is what you need the feather for, not me. If I were interested to go, there would always be other ways. There are often human beings of your kind who open up passageways for us.'

Gavin was too pre-occupied to hear the message. If she had no intention to use the feather as he'd thought she would, would it be just a test for him? 'Then, what do you need it for?'

'That's none of your business.' The witch snapped.

'I'm sorry. I don't mean to give any offense . . . I'm just curious . . . I mean curious to know more about you.' Fearing the witch would stop bargaining with him, Gavin tried to explain. But actually he'd become really interested to know more about the witch when he said so.

His sincere look did soften her. She hadn't expected to have talked so much with Gavin and now she had to go on. Living in solitude for hundreds of years, the witch was quite used to talking with only her plants and toads. They gave responses but they never asked questions. Once in a blue moon, the witch would meet humans and other creatures. They came to beg and bargain. None of them showed interest in her or dared to ask about her business. She hadn't cared because she had never wished or even thought about having someone to really talk to. But the arrival of the princess aroused something hidden. The princess was sincere with her, sharing her joy, her family, her dreams and her fears. In her heart, the witch was glad to have the princess trying to converse with her. But when the witch tried to respond, she found out that she couldn't recall anything about her family or her dream to share. Realizing that some part of her life was missing kept the witch from talking with the princess about any other personal things. The witch couldn't face the possibility that she would enjoy conversing with someone who was going to lose her past because of her.

For a minute, the witch just kept staring at Gavin and Gavin was scared to ask further. What was the harm in sharing her secret with this man from somewhere? So far, they had had a good conversation. The witch hadn't expected it but somehow she felt good.

Since the witch was not giving any response, Gavin just kept his mouth shut to avoid angering her further. He was too scared to look at her directly but from the corner of his eyes Gavin could see the witch slowly recovering her confident grin. To his surprise, the witch had changed her mind.

'I'll be happy to satisfy your curiosity about an old witch. Witches die one day like the ordinary people who come to seek our help but I am not going to die. We have a long life to find means of keeping alive and I've found mine. With the body parts from five immortal creatures, I will be able to live forever, and live young and beautiful forever. A phoenix feather can well be the last ingredient for my potion.'

'The last? So you've got the other four?'

'Yes . . . the horn of a unicorn, the big toe of a troll, the wings of a fairy and the heart of a dragon.'

'Wings from a fairy and heart from a dragon!' Gavin exclaimed. He was worried about the safety of his friends.

'Well, each fell into my hands with its story. You seem really interested in stories. Why can't I satisfy you further? It's nearly a hundred year since I got the first one. An immortal dragon fell in love with a girl and wanted to become a human like her. I was more than happy to help. He agreed to give me his heart in exchange for my spell. Being heartless was good for him. It would free him from feeling the pain in case of an unachievable love. He kept staying close to the girl to admire her and protect her. They became friends. But without the heart, he was getting weaker and weaker. The girl took care of him and cried for him when he was dying. Her tears activated my spell on him and he was turned into a human being as he'd wished. She fell in love with him and they got married. They lively happily though their ever after was just a few more years. He had a weak heart and so do all his male descendants.'

'And King Egbert was one of them.' When Gavin wrote about his Mariana saving the young knight, he just mentioned him as the descendant of the heartless dragon. He hadn't created or learnt about his background. He couldn't resist his curiosity to uncover more stories. 'What about the wings?'

'The wings were from an arrogant flower fairy called Rosita who had wished to overthrow the fairy queen. She liked visiting the human world. She saw how inferior the magic of a flower fairy was. Being invisible, putting someone to sleep, relieving pain, communicating with other creatures—these were too trivial for her. She came to me for the secret of black magic and agreed to pay for it with her wings. She thought she would become higher and mightier than the queen. She wished to lead the fairies to the wider world and was ambitious to dominate it. Her magic became more powerful but she herself did not. Rosita gained no respect from her fellow fairies. She lost her beauty due to the practice of black magic. She lost her identity from the moment she replaced her wings with those of a moth. And finally, she lost the battle because she had no support. After Rosita's departure, all the roses in Fairyland withered. The queen sowed rose seeds again and let them grow in isolation from all the other flowers. As the rose bushes grew thicker and taller, the passageway to the human world was hidden and soon all the fairies completely forgot about the outside world.'

'What had happened to Rosita afterwards?'

'What should I care about such an unpopular creature? But I did hear about an imp with a pair of moth wings living in the dark forest. Has she run away from the world in shame or in anger? What happened to her is up to your imagination.'

While responding to Gavin, the witch had moved over to the hearth. She poked one of her crooked fingers into the open mouth of a snake statuette above the fireplace. A cat flap big enough for a tiger became visible near the bottom of the wall. It was around half a metre tall. The witch gestured Gavin to go over to it and he did. He squatted down and pushed the flap slightly forward until it was wide enough to reveal a flight of stairs on the other side, leading all the way down. He could see Mariana moving among some green stuff slithering across the floor.

Mariana was trapped among poisonous snakes. How was he going to get her away from this horrible place? Gavin followed the witch down the stairs. It was dim down there once the flap closed behind them. A candle on the wall was the only source of illumination. It took Gavin a short while to adapt to the darkness. 'You'll free her if I give you the feather?'

'If I can remain immortal and young forever, why should I need an inheritor? The blood vow will be broken and then she will be free to go. She will resume her original appearance and of course lose all the dark power. It's a pity to lose her though. She has the instinct to communicate with my dear greenies.' It was a pity to lose her companion but another ugly witch without sympathy was not the kind of companion she wished for.

By the time the witch was saying her last sentence, she'd reached the bottom of the flight of stairs which led to the centre of the room. She was now standing by Mariana's side, among those green 'snakes' which twisted this way and that with the black butterflies in their midst. Gavin was only halfway down the stairs but he could see better now. They were not snakes but huge rope like vines with thorns. Just when Gavin felt them less threatening than snakes, the vines had sensed the intrusion of a stranger. They were crawling swiftly towards Gavin's legs.

'Move back!' Mariana was crying out to warn Gavin, who backed off a few steps, just in time to miss being caught by one of the vines. The young witch then whistled a tune to calm the agitated vines and the butterflies were once again flying among them.

In the meantime, the witch seemed to have dug out something from under the vines. Gavin couldn't see what it was or if she was really holding something. It wasn't until she came near him and moved one hand over the other as if she was opening something that Gavin could figure out it was a box in her hand. Gavin should have recognized the box wrapped in chameleon skin that was almost invisible unless one was aware of its presence, size and shape. The witch showed him the opened box, the inside of which was lined with fine silk. 'Now give me my last ingredient, the phoenix feather.'

Gavin looked into the box. The witch had not been lying. The other ingredients were there, occupying four different partitions. One empty partition was there, awaiting the feather. 'What makes you think I have the feather?'

'If you have been looking for something for almost a hundred years, you'll sense it when it's getting near.'

'Desire can distort your senses.'

'Should I take it as the advice from a survivor of such distortion?'

Gavin gave no response to the witch's mocking. But he did realize now that desire had distorted his judgment. He shouldn't have come, neither to the story world nor to the witch's place. Was he going to get through this?

The witch continued, 'The phoenix had never come to my mind before since the mythical bird rarely appeared in the area. Then recently I had a dream. I saw a feather glowing in the hands of someone who kept failing to draw a doorway with it.'

'But that was in Fairyland?'

'Yes, it was. So . . . .'

' . . . so since dreaming minds can take the body form there, I should have seen you.'

'Don't forget, witches can transfigure themselves. I don't think you or any of your fairy friends had paid attention to a Green Shield Bug camouflaging itself on a Bauhinia leaf.'

'You could have easily taken it away from me then.'

'Yes, like all other witches of your imagination. But I don't play those games. I don't trick. I trade. Besides, who else can you turn to if the feather's magic doesn't work for you? I knew you would come to me for one reason or another.'

'But our problem is I don't have it anymore.'

25

So the feather is with you

Periwinkle told Long and Zoe everything. Though the two had thought of the possibility of their story actually happening to Gavin, it was at this moment that they were certain it had. But they hadn't written Gavin going to the witch. What was the story there? Periwinkle had no idea what had happened to him after her departure either. She hoped Gavin was still fine.

Long was touching his feather affectionately. Its colour had faded a lot. He could go back to the bamboo jungle or to the mansion in Nanjing right now. But he knew Gavin needed him. He wasn't unaware of the possibility that the feather might lose its magic with just one more use. Long was ready to take the risk even though it meant a chance that both Gavin and he would be trapped in the story world. Worst still, he would be there alone if it turned out Gavin had been killed by the witch. But he might well be the only chance for Gavin to come home.

Zoe was ready to go and meet her daddy in the story world. She was excited to meet other characters and see the setting she had created. She had also thought of the worst. But even if she couldn't return, at least she would still be with her dad. It wouldn't be worse than being left here by herself. 'Come on, let's go.'

'I think your dad may not want you to go with us. It's too dangerous.' Long was also worrying about his feather failing him but he decided to keep this to himself.

'But I'm not scared.'

'I know you're brave and more than that, you're wise. You should be able to see the trouble you cause your dad. If you fall in the hands of the witch, she can threaten your dad for anything.'

'But perhaps the witch is not a bad one . . . or I can . . .' Zoe tried to argue. In her heart, she knew she wasn't scared to go only because she knew her dad would be there. She would have to depend on him.

'There is little you can do there. But you may be able to help if you stay behind. Keep writing. We may need your magic from here.' Long knew that Zoe would like to play a role.

'I can't write without your inspiration.'

'You can. You're the one who's been telling the story.'

'I need you to come back for the illustrations.'

'Yes, I will. You're the incentive for me and your dad to return. We'll fight whatever obstacles there are to come back because we know you're waiting.'

Zoe knew Long was right so she made up her mind and gave him a goodbye hug. 'Promise me you'll bring him back. Actually I'm not that brave. I'm scared I'll be left alone.'

'You know, you're the most courageous person I've ever met. You choose to face your fear. Both your dad and I have been running away from ours.'

Periwinkle gave Zoe the dreamosemary. 'Put it under your pillow. Have a good sleep if you lack any inspiration. Dreams will help.'

It was a nightmare for Gavin to be left alone in the dark basement with just the dim candle light. He was not tied up but neither could he leave nor move freely. The flap at the top of the stairs had disappeared since the witch and Mariana had left through it. The vines were crowding the whole room so that he could only stay up on the stairs. He had to keep backing off since the vines were really growing fast. Gavin was already at the top of the stairs but some vines had already grown long enough to reach him. Luckily, Gavin had a sword so he just kept swinging it to chop off those trying to grab him. But he wouldn't dare to move all the way down since the vines at the bottom were much denser and they could approach from all directions. He couldn't tell how long this threatening scenario had lasted but this heavy lifting with the sword was tiring him out as if he had gone through it for hours and hours. He couldn't spare any attention to think of a better solution. But one thought remained—the question of whether Periwinkle had found Long and Zoe. Gavin had trusted that Long would come to bring him home but at this moment, he wished he wouldn't. At least one person could return home. That would be better than two being killed.

'So the feather is with you.'
Long couldn't see or hear the witch, who was just by his side, admiring the feather in his hand. In the eyes of the witch, the feather was as colourful and beautiful as she

had imagined or when she last saw it in Gavin's hands. But Long could see the changes. He had seen it when it was much brighter and its colours shone. Long just kept wishing it could work one more time so to bring Gavin back to Zoe. He dared not to ask for more as he felt that it would be too greedy.

'We can't just keep waiting. Let's go into the wood and find Gavin before it gets dark.' Long wasn't going to follow Periwinkle's instruction.

Periwinkle was supposed to keep Long from getting into any danger that Gavin might not escape from. They were supposed to wait outside till sunset. If Gavin couldn't get out by then, Long should leave without him, go back to his own world. But Periwinkle supported Long's decision. If he was going to abandon Gavin after waiting for a few more hours, he wouldn't have chosen to come in the first place. 'Yes, the sooner we get to Gavin, the greater chance we have to save him. Let's go!'

'Save him . . . from what? Me?' Of course, the witch knew how people thought about her. 'I'll wait for you.'

Once after Long and Periwinkle had vanished in front of her eyes, Zoe returned to the writing pad. For one reason, she really hoped that her writing could help. Another reason was she needed something to keep her mind occupied. Though her dad had been missing over a day, it was now that she was really alone. For the first time, Zoe felt scared. So she kept herself busy with the writing. She continued the story with what had actually happened according to Periwinkle's narrative. She also added more details to previously written parts. So far her dad was a hero and above all, she hoped that he was still safe despite the dangers. She knew he was. She was sure, or was she?

But the temporary relief of this train of thought finally came to an end when Zoe got to the scene of her dad confronting the witch. She could choose to imagine it going on smoothly, say the witch agreed to free the princess in exchange for his sword. But she found it hard to persuade herself that things had actually happened as she was about to write now. She was forced to face her worry as she speculated on other possibilities, most of which were negative. But Zoe had no wish to stop writing the story. She wished to go ahead of what was happening now. In this way, she could write to direct what might happen afterwards.

If only she could know what was happening now . . . wait . . . that leaf which Periwinkle gave her. It might bring her to her dad in a dream.

Light began to leak into the room through the outline of the flap appearing in its former place. As the flap was pushed open, more light flooded in but it disappeared soon after Mariana had entered. She walked by Gavin and put something in his hands while whispering in his ears, 'Chew and swallow them at once!' He could feel from the texture that they were flowers but he was not able to distinguish the colours in the dim light. He put them in his mouth without a question or the need for a second thought. Things couldn't be worse even the flowers were poisonous. The witches could have killed him easily by any means but he just trusted his instinct that this was the same Mariana who had warned him from the thorny vines. The flowers were a little bitter and slightly cool so he imagined he was just chewing some mint leaves. The association with something edible made it less awful to chew and swallow them.

After giving Gavin the flowers, Mariana continued her way down the stairs. She hadn't stopped to see if he was following her instruction. She was confident he would. She was carrying a big cage to the vines at the bottom. The butterflies followed her and were happy to be among the vines again. She opened the cage and hundreds of rats came running out of it. The vines were now busy catching the rats.

'Help, daddy!' Zoe jumped and screamed as the rats ran past and through her legs. Before Zoe ran to her dad, she had already realized that it was a nightmare. No. It wasn't a nightmare. It was a dream, a dream she had wished for. She tried to cover her mouth to stop herself from yelling. She was afraid she would wake herself up. Her hand couldn't feel her mouth but anyway it wasn't necessary for she couldn't hear her screams. Slowly, she began moving towards Gavin. She walked carefully at first among the sweeping vines and after realizing that her steps weren't bothering the vines, she ran as fast as she could. She jumped onto her dad as she always did. She fell but it didn't hurt. She tried to poke and touch Gavin but her fingers went through his arm. Finally Zoe had to accept the fact that she was now nothing more than the surrounding air. But she was content just to stand next to her dad and watch what he was watching. From this new position, the young witch, who was previously behind her, was first to catch her eye. At once, Zoe recognized her as her princess.

Within a minute, the vines had got all the rats. Once a rat was caught, that vine would retreat back to the far end corner of the basement whence it seemed to originate. Tracing its path, Gavin and Zoe could now see a green gigantic flower there. It was almost three times the size of a normal human head. But it had remained so still compared to the highly active vines that Gavin hadn't noticed the flower until now. One by one, the rats were dropped down into the flower, the petals of which then closed to consume its prey.

'Yuck!' Zoe exclaimed.

Gavin now knew what his fate would have been if he hadn't got the sword. But now Mariana was gesturing to him to come down to her. It was easier for him to swallow the flowers with unsure consequence than it was for him to move towards a foreseen danger, especially after he had witnessed how horrible it was to be torn up by a blood stained flower.

'Go, she was my princess. She won't hurt you.' Zoe knew he couldn't hear her but she was used to speak her mind. She was quick to act as well. While Gavin was still hesitating, she was already sitting next to Mariana.

'Come. They won't bother you.' Mariana was trying to keep her voice down.

Zoe nodded.

Gavin wasn't sure why but he went. To his surprise, even though he was standing in the midst of the vines, they just ignored him.

'The flower you ate was emitting a scent to fool them.' Mariana explained when he sat down next to her.

'Daddy, you're sitting on me.' Zoe complained and moved away even though she didn't feel anything. She settled herself opposite to Gavin and Mariana so she could see their every move.

'That scent is beyond the threshold humans can distinguish.' Mariana chuckled when she saw Gavin sniffing himself.

Zoe burst into laughter also. And laughing like this, she realized it was just one day he'd been gone but at this moment, she felt she was missing him so much.

'Are you eating those flowers, too?'

'No, the greenies are my pets.'

Now Gavin could see the difference. The vines ignored him but were actually winding around Mariana's arms and body like pet snakes. They were slithering on her lap and by her side, hoping for attention and gentle touches.

'Where is the witch?'

'She's taking a nap. She's trying to locate the feather in her dream.'

'I'm back!'

Zoe raised her head to the voice and saw the witch at the foot of the stairs, walking towards them. Zoe's first reaction was to pull Gavin to go but her failing grasp reminded her that she was invisible.

The witch had moved closer now and Zoe could see her face better. She looked extremely ugly, so ugly that she would never forget her face.

'So she didn't believe that I dropped the feather in the ravine?' Gavin rose up and stood in front of Mariana.

'Of course, not.' Mariana replied calmly and in a soft voice while she kept patting the vines gently.

Zoe was surprised to see them go on talking even though the witch was beside them watching. Then Zoe realized that they couldn't see the witch. And then she knew that the witch must have got there by dreaming too. But she could see the witch. So it meant that the witch might see her as well. Zoe looked at the witch. She looked back and was smiling at her.

'So that's why she is keeping me here. She hasn't killed me because she wants to use me to bargain for the feather in case a friend has been keeping it for me.' Gavin began pacing around Mariana as he put forward his speculation. He even knocked against the witch but she kept her position and her smile.

'What makes you think that she would like to kill you?' Mariana didn't rise. She just raised her head to look at Gavin.

' . . . because I'm an ugly, old witch.' The witch was the one giving the answer but she was actually talking to Zoe.

'What's the difference if she will turn me into a rock as she has done to the dragon or dissolve my limbs or . . .' Gavin was quite agitated.

'The difference is a curse can be broken.' Mariana put down the vines that had been playing in her lap and stood to face Gavin.

The witch was nodding.

'But she's leaving me here to be eaten by those horrible flowers.'

'Are you to be eaten? She would have taken away your sword then.'

The witch kept nodding and so did Zoe.

Then the witch turned to Zoe. 'I have to go now. I'm glad to have met you.' The witch disappeared but her voice went on for a further short while, 'They'll give me the feather . . .'

'No! . . . ' Zoe yelled back.

26

Why should I save him?

' . . . without it, he can't come home.' Zoe woke up crying out at the top of her voice. So was it just a dream or was it actually happening in the story world? Real or not, Zoe decided to build on it. She felt much inspired and she couldn't stop writing. Now with the real image of the witch in her mind, she made up the missing part. She wrote about her demand for the feather to free the princess. And the only motive Zoe could think for her was that the magic of the feather could help to restore her youth and beauty. Then it came to the part she had witnessed though she skipped the fact of herself and the witch having been there. What was going to happen next? Zoe was confident she could write to make things happen especially after she had met the princess who looked exactly the same as Zoe had created. Her black butterflies were just as real. Zoe was determined to help through writing her story.

The witch woke up as one of her toads was licking her face from the other end of her hammock with its extraordinary long tongue. It had even caught a fly on its way. 'So he's here?' The witch asked as she got down from her dirty ragged hammock, crowded with frogs and toads.

Together, her slimy and warty friends croaked to mean yes. They could sense the vibration of the ground when someone was still over a hundred metres away. The witch nodded with a grin and made her way back into the cottage. She liked sleeping in the garden in their company but she preferred to wait for her guest inside. Her little green friends dispersed and vanished among the grass and trees after she'd gone. There was a spell to stop them from entering.

As Mariana was patting the thorny vines gently, they felt into a nap. 'Now before the greenies wake up, you should leave at once. Come this way.' Saying so Mariana had got up, took Gavin by the hand and led him through the vines. The butterflies were flying after them. The swarm took the shape of the mouse cage as they crowded on it to lift it along. The basement was not big but Gavin and Mariana had to inch forward to avoid stepping on any of the vines or touching the thorns. Finally, they were at the corner guarded by the giant flower. 'That's the way out.' Mariana pointed to the wall behind the flower.

'The wall?'

'Down there, just behind the flower. See the big spider web. There's a long tunnel behind it, leading all the way out.

Bending lower, now Gavin could see a densely woven spider web at the foot of the wall though most part of it was blocked by the flower. It couldn't be much bigger than half a metre in diameter. He could see no light in it so it had to run for quite a distance underground before it led out to anywhere.

'Where is it leading to?'

'I don't know. The witch has never mentioned it.'

'Then how did you find out about it?'

Mariana got the floating mouse cage down from the butterflies. From inside, she took out a book that Gavin couldn't see at first until it was waved in front of his eyes—a book wrapped in chameleon skin.

'Your book?' Gavin was surprised to see the book. He remembered he had put it in the package on the dragon's back. It was part of the stone statue now.

'Not mine. It belongs to the witch. Her name was Kathleen. I found it just this morning when I fed the greenies. It might have been buried here for over a hundred years. It might have even been exposed for a long time as the vines kept dragging the surface soil here and there over the years. It was just never noticed because of its camouflage and especially since the vines got denser and denser. Kathleen must have gone through the same struggles as I have. She had thought of the same solutions but she had long forgotten about the book . . . and the tunnel.'

Mariana handed the book to Gavin. He turned to the last written page which showed a picture of a hole at the foot of the wall. A big cross was drawn on it. But unlike previous pages, there was no written text to go with the picture.

'But why was it crossed out? It may not lead anywhere.'

'It's still worth trying . . .

". . . It may get you out of the wood." said the Princess.

Gavin knew that his friend Long would have come already. Periwinkle and Long should be waiting for him outside the wood. If he acted at once, he would soon be home. But he was worried about the princess. "When the witch finds out that you let me go, she will be angry with you and kill you."

"She won't. She has forgotten about the secret way. When she finds out you're missing, she will think that you have been eaten up by the giant flower. Now go at once." Gavin gave the Princess a hug and said goodbye.'

Zoe was shaking her right hand as she read over what she had written. She felt much inspired that she had been writing fast and non-stop. She could write another story to save her princess and Witch Kathleen, perhaps getting a feather from the phoenix that Long had drawn to life from the roof statue. If everything turned out as she had written, she would see her daddy soon.

Zoe read again what she had on the paper before her. A tunnel leading to outside where Long could meet Gavin and bring him home. It could save her dad but she just didn't like the plot.

Not long after the witch had settled herself at the tree trunk table with a bowl of hot soup, she heard Long at the door. Without bothering to put down the soup, she raised the dripping spoon to point to the door. The door swung open with its usual squeak just before Long would have knocked on it.

'Come in!' Long heard the witch calling out so he dropped the idea of still knocking. He stepped in. With another squeak, the door was closed behind him. Long wasn't intimidated by the dim and shabby environment at all. He had experienced similar living conditions before. He wasn't frightened by the grotesque look of the witch or bothered by her mouldy odour either. Long could remember those contemptuous expressions thrown at him when he was begging on the street. He felt sympathy for the witch but he would treat her courteously just as he did to anybody else. With no fear, no pity and no flattery, Long walked closer to the witch and gave her a bow. 'Good afternoon, lady.'

The Green Fingered Witch was quite impressed by his politeness and sincerity. 'Have a seat, young man.' She pointed to the protruding part of a tree root opposite to hers. She then raised her head in the direction Periwinkle was flying. 'And you, little fairy.' Periwinkle had been looking around for Gavin since she flew in.

Long sat down as instructed. Periwinkle followed and sat on his shoulder though she kept turning her head and looking around.

Long waited patiently when the witch was busy with the fire and getting him a bowl of soup. The witch appreciated his patience. Finally she settled down in her seat after offering Long a bowl of soup.

'Lady, I'm sorry to come and bother you. I'm looking for a friend named Gavin . . .'

'Try the soup!' The witch interrupted Long. She took a sip of hers and looked at Long.

Periwinkle was shaking her head but Long tried the soup to show his trust. The witch was pleased and asked 'What can I do to help you?'

'I know Gavin should have come to ask you for some help. I'd like to know where he is now. I've promised his daughter to bring him home.'

'He's here, in my basement.'

'Can he go home with me?'

'Sure, but only if you leave the phoenix feather behind.'

'I will, once after I draw the doorway for Gavin.'

Mariana and Gavin were kneeling behind the dormant flower, trying to wipe the dense and sticky spider web away. It wasn't as easy as it appeared. Finally, they could see a gap big enough to crawl through.

'Wait! Take the book. She would have wished her spells able to be undone. You'll need it to save the dragon too.'

Gavin retreated a step and reached up to get the book from Mariana, and while he did so the vines began moving actively again as light leaked in with the appearance of the flap. The sudden actions of the vines had wakened the flower. It was turning towards Gavin, revealing its smelly, bloodthirsty hollow in the centre. Gavin was really scared now, partly because of its horrible look, even though it wasn't attacking yet, and partly because he knew the witch would be coming any second. He would not be able to escape if he didn't act fast. He drew the sword, knowing the threat of the flower had to be ended.

'No, don't hurt it. Just go.' Before Mariana could stop him, Gavin had lopped the flower's head off in one blow.

Immediately, the vines turned into all kinds of snakes. Their scales were shining and so were their eyes and fangs. Light flooded in with the open flap. In came the witch, Long and Periwinkle. They were stunned to see the snakes crowded around Gavin.

Gavin was too scared to move. He knew there was no chance that he could run away from the hundreds of snakes in front of him. But at the moment the snakes were keeping an arm's length from him, just hissing and staring at him. Except a few slithering to and fro, most remained quite still at their positions.

Mariana first tried whistling the tune that had worked to calm the vines before. But the snakes ignored her totally. She knew they were not her greenies anymore. She tried some milder spells but they didn't work either. They were not ordinary snakes. When she was saying the petrification spell, something black but reflective like a mirror flew just in front of her to block her view of the snakes. She would have petrified herself if the green fingered witch had not been quick enough to push the 'mirror' away. It dispersed into a swamp of flying creatures.

'My butterflies?' Mariana exclaimed.

'Not any more. They've turned back to imps.' The witch sighed as she took out a marble from under her sleeve. She threw the marble on the ground, but it landed as a big crystal ball, the size of a watermelon.

'What happened?' Mariana asked.

'Shouldn't you be the one to tell me?' The witch snapped. She was taking out a small flask from the other sleeve and she emptied the potion onto the crystal ball. At once, the ball glowed in the dim room and all the imps rushed to it, penetrated through the crystal film and were trapped inside. They were ugly, bald creatures with torn leathery black wings, skinny bodies around the size of a small finger. They had spindly limbs, angular faces, narrow red eyes and pointy ears. They were now pressing against the crystal wall from the inside, knocking, kicking, pushing, sticking out their black tongues and showing their saw-edged teeth.

Meanwhile, the anxious Long and Periwinkle had come down to join the others. The snakes turned just to give the newcomers a threatening look and then resumed their attention in Gavin's direction. Gavin remained still and so did the snakes. He was aware that the snakes were interested only in him so he dared not say anything in case that might trigger some new onslaught on their part. He could only use his eyes to thank Long for coming.

After taking care of the imps, the witch was dashing towards Gavin without any attempt to avoid stepping on the snakes. They moved submissively aside to let her pass.

'Be patient! We just need a few more minutes to shed our old skins.' A boa constrictor was hissing to stop a cobra which had just spread its hood in anger. They knew that after the long rest, their power would double once their new selves popped out from the old skins. But during this moulting stage, they were at their weakest so they tried to remain still.

'You wouldn't want to be trapped like the imps.' A rattlesnake was insisting.

'They were friends, trying to save us just now.' Though the boa also felt the imps were a bit impulsive, he did appreciate their partnership.

'Sh, sh . . . the man seems to be listening to us.' The rattlesnake rattled his tail.

Long was trying to hear what the snakes were hissing to each other. He could understand his animal friends in the bamboo jungle. But the snakes were whispering so softly that he couldn't hear them too well.

Periwinkle was listening, too and she could hear them. She just pretended she wasn't listening. She was thinking of the sleeping dust in her pocket but she knew it would not be strong enough.

'Can you save Gavin?' Long whispered to Periwinkle.

'I'm still thinking.' But she didn't look confident.

Long knew the witch was their only chance since he could see that the crawling creatures were quite scared of her. 'Would you please save Gavin from the snakes?' Long begged anxiously.

'Why should I save someone who killed my flower?' The witch howled and threw a fierce look at Gavin. She picked up the chopped flower gently and she looked really sad. It had accompanied her for hundreds of years.

Gavin could feel her grief and he was sorry to have caused it. He had never thought before that he could be the source of others' sufferings. He never meant to be but things could happen. 'I'm so sorry. I shouldn't have . . .'

The witch didn't want to listen to him. She just grabbed the sword from Gavin's hand and the next moment it was pointed towards him.

27

He can go through that tunnel

'You can't kill him! He's the one!' shouted the imps who had already settled inside the crystal ball. They didn't seem to worry too much of being trapped. It was as if they knew they would soon get out of it. The power of the crystal ball wouldn't last long and the monster snakes would soon gain control.

The witch threw the sword down. She was just trying to scare him. The sword fell onto something—her book. She could see it as there were the stains of some flower juice on the cover. The imps and snakes before her eyes had stirred up some of her memory and she seemed to recognize the book as something belonging to her. She picked it up and flipped over the pages.

The snakes were hissing again and Long could hear them this time.

'That man thinks we are going to hurt this man.' A green viper was whispering to its neighbour.

'Why should we hurt the man who has saved us?'

'What are we waiting for? Let's get him out from here.' An orange corn snake joined in the conversation.

'Don't worry! The snakes were not going to hurt you.' Long comforted Gavin with what he had overheard.

'So you can hear their conversation, too?' Periwinkle was surprised that Long also had their fairy talent to communicate with other living creatures. But she was sure Long hadn't heard what she had heard from the cobra and the boa before otherwise he wouldn't have believed these cunning snakes now.

'Yes. I think I can communicate with them.' Long became more confident now. Perhaps the best way to free Gavin was to talk to the snakes directly so he squatted down to address the snakes. 'Thank you for trying to help my friend. Can he go now?'

'Yes, he can go through that tunnel.' A rattlesnake pointed its rattling tail to the hole behind Gavin.

'They're trying to trick you. Whatever it says, don't do it!' Periwinkle warned Long.

'What did it say?' Mariana and Gavin asked.

'My friend is advising you to go through that tunnel.' The boa was now speaking in human language that they could understand. The skin of its snaky face was torn open and out emerged a scaly reddish brown face that looked something between a man and a snake. A nose became obvious and the cheeks bones were more protruding. The face was longer with a bearded chin. But the mouth was lipless and wide, extending from one ear to another and still with its forked tongue. The eyes were disproportionally big compared to those on a human face and they sparkled creepily in the dark. As the skin continued to tear off down the body, a pair of arms began to emerge. Gavin and the others could expect that soon all the snakes would mutate into such monsters.

But by now the witch had read through the book and she remembered everything. Her name was Kathleen. She had been ambitious to lead in the world of black magic so as to make use of such unbeatably destructive forces against the evils. But as her dark power increased, she couldn't keep her mind untouched by the dark force. The last thing she did before she lost her mind totally was to safeguard the tunnel from the dark creatures which had discovered its existence. The tunnel was leading to other worlds. But the passageway between any two worlds would be opened only after an accidental intruder from that world returned home through it. The imps and the snake monsters were keeping their eyes on the tunnel. They knew the chance was there otherwise such an opening would not have existed. The young Witch Kathleen had shared the same belief but she was determined to prevent the evil force from leaking into any other world. She won over the imps and snakes with the giant flower she had cultivated to capture the spirits of the dark creatures. After that, the imps were transfigured into the tamed black butterflies and the snakes were captivated as the vines to serve the giant flower. Before Kathleen could record anything further than just marking a cross on the picture of the tunnel, she had forgotten everything. If that sword hadn't been made to break a wizard's spell, it wouldn't have been powerful enough to chop down the flower. The spell on the snakes and imps might have lasted forever.

'No, you mustn't go through that tunnel. You can't afford the consequences once you have opened the way for these evils to get into your world.'

'The world is big. Forget about it. You just need to think about going home—your home.' The boa-monster coaxed.

'He has his own way to go home.' Saying so, the witch waved her left sleeve and a strong wind blew Gavin to Long's side. 'Draw the door and leave at once.' She had to act fast before all the snakes turned into their monster forms. She wouldn't be strong enough to fight them all at the same time.

By now Periwinkle and Mariana had joined her. Periwinkle with her sleeping dust and Mariana with whatever powerful spells she could think of, helped to impede the actions of some snakes. At the same time, Witch Kathleen's green fingers were getting longer and longer. They were glowing and as she raised her hand, snowflakes began to sprinkle down. She was fighting with great determination.

After Zoe had finished writing the story, she sat in front of the wall through which she had witnessed Long and Periwinkle departing. She was expecting her dad and Long to come back through the same way. Fifteen minutes had passed. Maybe it took some time. She read her story again.

' . . . Within a few minutes, the snow was falling heavily and the witch was gaining the upper hand. Finally, the imps were trapped inside a snow globe with ever falling snow. They looked prettier now their wings were glowing, coated with snow. The snake monsters trying to attack from all directions were frozen into ice statues in different postures and in the midst of various actions . . .' Zoe liked the idea she had from her favourite snow globe and the collectible figure toys.

*"The imps were trapped inside a snow globe and
the snake monsters were frozen into ice statutes."*

It was another fifteen minutes but they were not back yet.
'Did the fight take so long?' She read her last paragraph again
to make sure it was alright.

'... While the witches and the fairy were fighting with the
imps and snake monsters, Long had drawn the doorway back
to Gavin's study. Long kept his promise and left the feather for
the witch. After shouting a goodbye to Witch Kathleen, the
princess and Periwinkle, Gavin and Long walked through the
door ...'

'It's really good, right? It's exciting. We've got monsters
and dangers. The witch isn't bad so she deserves the feather.
Long can't return to the jungle but it's even better. He can
stay with us. The best part is they will be home.' Zoe was still
talking to herself since Long and Gavin were still not here. She
was so keen to share with them her feeling that she couldn't
wait to hold it just in mind.

While the witches and the fairy were fighting with the imps and snake monsters, Long was trying to draw the doorway to Gavin's study. The feather lost its lustre completely after a few strokes.

'What took you so long?' The witch yelled to ask. 'We can't keep things up much longer.'

Long knew the feather had lost its magic but he kept trying. He knew it had to be a miracle but a miracle had to work through something. He had promised Zoe to bring her dad back. *But sorry Zoe, it's not working.* Gavin could tell from Long's expression that he had tried his best. He gently patted Long's shoulder to let him know he should stop.

Within a few minutes, the snow was falling heavily and the witch was gaining the upper hand. Finally, the imps were trapped inside a snow globe with ever falling snow. They looked prettier now their wings were glowing, coated with snow. The snake monsters trying to attack from all directions were frozen into ice statues in different postures and in the midst of various actions . . .

Then almost at the same time the two men from two different ages and two different worlds shared the same feeling.

'Zoe was writing our story.' Gavin cried out suddenly. 'Look at that crystal ball trapping the imps. It's exactly like the snow globe I gave her last Christmas, only that hers had fairies instead of imps.'

'And those ice statutes. She's got one today from that monster . . . how to call it . . . eh, toy vending machine.' Long noticed the same thing too.

'She bought another one? She's got a lot of those figure toys.'

'Yes, she's shown me part of her collection.'

Both men's hearts were lightened now that they spoke of Zoe.

Why are you so happy? You are trapped here.' Mariana felt anxious for them after seeing their attempt to go home had failed.

'The snow will melt soon. We can't trap them forever.' The witch had a further worry about the snake monsters attacking them. She wouldn't be powerful enough to fight against them when all the snakes turned into their monster forms. They would keep moulting once they were free from the ice.

But we're in a fairy tale. The good guys will win. Gavin believed it not because he was a fairy tale writer but because he believed in his daughter. *Little princess, I can feel you behind us.*

Yes, if we stop believing in it, there'll be no magic. Long had got his idea from Zoe.

Both men were thinking of Zoe. If there are tunnels going between worlds, why shouldn't there be channels to communicate across time and space? Looking at the tunnel, they were thinking of the same thing. *There can be magic elsewhere.*

Zoe was tired of talking to herself but the conversation had made her think of something. Why couldn't she call to talk to her dad and Long? She called from her heart and was soon connected. At least, she believed so.

'Hey, daddy, can you hear me?'

'Yes, little princess! I can feel you behind us.'

'Is Long with you?'

'He is and he has tried his best.'
'Sorry Zoe, but it's not working anymore.'

'The feather? I know something must have gone wrong . . . . But there can be magic elsewhere.'

Feeling she had spoken with them, Zoe picked up her pen and continued her writing.

'Let's try the tunnel!' Gavin suggested. 'That might be our only chance.'

'That would open the way for the evils to your world.' Mariana felt she must stop them.

'Yes, Zoe won't like that to happen . . . so she won't let it happen.' Long was confident.

'Go at once! Take the tunnel!' The Green Fingered Witch had changed her mind. She knew it must have been there for a purpose.

'But when the snow melts . . .' Mariana looked at the witch in disbelief. *She has been guarding it for so many years.*

'I'm just a witch. Why should I bother guarding another world?' The witch knew that the monstrous snakes and imps wouldn't bother her either once that tunnel was opened. She turned to Long, 'Just give me the feather as you've promised and you are free to leave my place whatever way you like.'

Long gave the feather a last gentle touch from one end to the other. He then handed it to the witch, hoping that it could still serve her purpose.

'Now go, one by one!' Witch Kathleen pointed to the tunnel. 'It will take each of you back to your own homes.' Before she finished her words, she had turned away from them to go and fetch her box.

'My home.' Long had almost forgotten he had his own in the bamboo jungle. He had his old friends waiting for him there. If only he could have more time, he had much to say to his new friends but now all he could say was goodbye. He wouldn't even have the chance to say goodbye to Zoe.

Gavin was ready to go. He gave the sword to Princess Mariana. 'Would you please take this to the dragon and ask him to keep it for me.' He was sure Witch Kathleen wouldn't leave the dragon a statue. He was just not sure if the feather could fulfill her wish that Princess Mariana could be free from her now. He looked up in Periwinkle's direction to say goodbye to her. 'See you again in my dream!' Lastly, he gave Long a brotherly grip on his upper arm. 'Thank you!'

Long gave a bow to Gavin. 'Tell Zoe I'll miss her.' Then he climbed into that big hole leading to the tunnel without turning back. He knew that this was the end of a memorable journey.

Following Long, Gavin climbed into the hole. In front of him was the long tunnel, the end of which was not in sight. He couldn't see Long in front of him either though they weren't even a minute apart.

' . . . Gavin and Long climbed into the hole. It was a long, dark tunnel which was getting narrower and smaller as they moved through it. Soon they were crawling on all fours but not long after that, they could feel some fresh air and started seeing light ahead of them. After a short while, the light source was over their heads. They climbed up a hole and found themselves in the middle of a street where the constructors had newly dug up the road surface for underground pipe maintenance. Gavin and Long were back in the real world . . .'

Before Zoe had put down her pen, the doorbell rang. It was faster than she had expected. She rushed to open the door and the next second, she was already in her dad's arms, overjoyed with tears. There was so much to tell from both sides but for over a minute the only words father and daughter shared were 'I missed you so much!'

Epilogue

'Where's Long?'

'He should be home in the bamboo jungle.'

'But that's not what I wrote.'

'. . . .'

Gavin couldn't explain it either. It would take some time for Zoe to accept that Long had returned to his own world. It would take even longer to understand how dangerous it would be if one could always make things happen as one wished, even in another world.

Zoe wasn't sure now if things would happen as she wrote but she wished for that possibility. So she finished her story with . . .

. . . When Gavin and Long were entering the tunnel, Witch Kathleen had already put the feather together with the four other treasures in a cauldron. She said a magic spell as she stirred the ingredients over a greenish flame. Everything melted into a potion. It could make Witch Kathleen young and beautiful forever but she didn't take it. She poured it on the giant flower. Immediately, it came back to life. Just before the imps and snake monsters could regain their power, the giant flower had captivated them once again.

Kathleen and Mariana remained witches but they were good witches. People liked them because they only practiced the good magic. They let children ride on their brooms. They made potions for people to find true love and to get cured from sickness and wounds.

The dragon was made a knight and was called Sir Dragon. He stayed to guard the white Castle but he didn't even fight once in a battle because it was a very peaceful kingdom. He was still keeping the sword, waiting for his hero to come and get it back.

Periwinkle returned to Fairyland. Sometimes she might explore across the rose bushes for fun but she always returned home. There was no better place than Fairyland.

Long came out from the tunnel under a limestone pool. Kit Kit and the other friends didn't even notice that he had disappeared for a day. They thought he was just playing hide and seek with them. Long would of course never forget the wonderful day he had spent with Zoe. If one day he could get another feather, he would for sure choose to visit her.

Zoe was quite optimistic about that.

I'm not sure if things won't happen somewhere at sometime as written? Hence, I am going to end my story with . . .

Gavin has returned to his profession as a surgeon. Through the incredible journey with his characters, he has recovered his courage and passion to move on. He believed Long should have too. Gavin ended his last published story, 'Long, the Talented Painter' with . . .

The magic of the feather had made Long realized how much he missed the place he belonged. He was ready to accept the past and face the future. He left his feather behind in a dream and returned to Nanjing, which though no longer the capital, was still as flourished as he last saw it. The talented young man became a famous artist and a travelling artist. So occasionally he would be back to the bamboo jungle to visit his friends and find new inspiration. He knew he didn't need any more magic to make his dream come true. He didn't draw only with what he saw or remembered but also what he could imagine. *Thanks for the inspiration, dear friends.*

Gavin is still making up fairy tales for Zoe and the orphans or sick children he meets in his volunteer work. But he doesn't write anymore. He says he doesn't have the time and that's true. As a devoted doctor and a responsible father, he really doesn't have much time for anything else.

But Zoe has taken up the writing. She is writing better and better and she believes she will be a writer one day. We may need to wait for some years to read her first book but her first story has been published—'The Witch Princess', illustrated by Long, was one of the collected stories under 'The Little Author Project'.

Would Long, Gavin and Zoe have another magic encounter? One can't be sure. But we know that both Gavin and Zoe still have some dreamosemary and we hope they will live happily ever after.

The End